KT-440-864

THE PRINCESS'S NEW YEAR WEDDING

REBECCA WINTERS

MILLS & BOON

First published in Great Britain 2019
by Mills & Boon, an imprint of HarperCollins*Publishers*
1 London Bridge Street, London, SE1 9GF

Large Print edition 2019

© 2019 Rebecca Winters

ISBN: 978-0-263-08244-9

MIX
Paper from
responsible sources
FSC™ C007454

This book is produced from independently certified
FSC™ paper to ensure responsible forest management. For
more information visit www.harpercollins.co.uk/green.

Printed and bound in Great Britain
by CPI Group (UK) Ltd, Croydon, CR0 4YY

How lucky was I to be born to
my darling, talented mother,
who was beautiful inside and out?

She filled my life with joy
and made me so happy to be alive!

I love you, Mom.

CHAPTER ONE

"*MIO FIGLIO?* I know it's early, but there are things I must talk to you about. *Come to the apartment.*"

Thirty-year-old Stefano sat up in bed. It was a shock to get a phone call from his father at 5:30 a.m., but his father's entreaty shocked him even more.

"You mean now?"

"Please."

"I'll be there as soon as I can."

Stefano realized his father's broken heart wouldn't allow him to sleep, but then Stefano doubted anyone in the palace had known a moment's rest for the past week. Alberto, his adored younger brother—his parents' beloved son and heir to the throne—had just been buried yesterday at the young age of twenty-eight. There was no antidote for sorrow.

Stefano's twenty-seven-year-old sister, Carla, and her husband, Dino, and two children, were just as grief-stricken over the loss of a wonderful brother and uncle. She was now first in line to the throne and would be queen when their father died or could no longer rule. The rules of succession fell to the firstborn, then the second or the third, regardless of gender.

Stefano would never rule.

Since his eighteenth birthday when he'd prevailed on his parents to be exempt from royal duty for the rest of his life, Stefano had been granted that exemption by parliament. From that time forward, he was no longer a royal, but he loved his family and they loved him. They'd all come together for this unexpected tragedy.

With Alberto gone, his mother looked like she'd aged twenty years and had gone to bed after the interment of her second-born son. The funeral had been too much for her.

Stefano had struggled with his pain and was forced to face the fact that he was now the *only* son of King Basilio. Though his father would rely more and more on Carla, he needed Stefano, too, and would lean on him for comfort. Stefano guessed that was why his father had summoned him this early in the morning. Forcing himself to move, Stefano dragged himself out of bed to shower and dress.

Before long he entered his parents' private lounge off their bedroom in the north wing of the palace. His bereaved father turned away from the fireplace to look at him. "Thank you for coming, Stefano. Your mother is still in bed, overcome with grief."

"As *you* are, *Papà*." Stefano gave him a soulful hug. It would be impossible to get over the reality that Alberto had been killed in a car crash a week ago.

Stefano, who'd graduated from the Colorado School of Mines in the US, had been in Canada at the time, inspecting one of the Casale gold mines. Casale being an old family name dating back to the founding of Italy. Nothing had seemed real until he'd returned home to the Kingdom of Umbriano, located in the Alps. His father had met him after the royal jet touched down and they went to identify Alberto's body.

Yesterday's state funeral in the basilica of Umbriano, presided over by the cardinal who had also delivered the eulogy, had been a great tribute to Alberto, a favorite son revered by the people. Dignitaries of many countries had attended, including of course the royal family of the Kingdom of Domodossola bordering France, Switzerland and Italy.

Stefano would never forget the vacant look on the face of Alberto's betrothed, Princess Lanza Rossiano of Domodossola, beneath her black, gauzy veil. He'd met war victims after serving a required year in the military in the Middle East who'd had that same lost, bewildered expression, their whole world wiped out.

The twenty-two-year-old daughter of King

Victor Emmanuel of Domodossola had been betrothed to Alberto twelve months ago. Their marriage was supposed to take place a year from now on New Year's Day, and her family had clearly been devastated.

Stefano, who was rarely in the country because of business, hadn't met with King Victor's family since his childhood when both families got together on occasion. Meeting them again at the funeral, he was shocked to see all three of the king's daughters grown up. Not until he witnessed their bereavement did Stefano realize how terrible the news must have been for them. Stefano still couldn't believe Alberto was gone.

"Sit down. We have something vital to discuss."

By vital, his father must mean he wanted Stefano to stay around for a while, but that would be impossible because of Stefano's latest gold mining project in Kenya. He needed to fly there the day after tomorrow to oversee a whole new gold processing invention that could bring in a great deal more money. Hopefully, it would serve as a prototype for all his other gold mines throughout the world. He imagined he'd be gone six weeks at least.

With his hands clasped between his legs, Stefano closed his eyes, knowing his father was in so much pain at the moment that he needed all their support, but he was curious as to what his father wanted to talk about.

"The wedding to Princess Lanza must go on as planned. Since losing Alberto, your mother and I have talked of nothing else. It's imperative that *you* take your brother's place."

Stefano's head jerked up. "Surely, I didn't hear you correctly."

"I know this comes as a shock to you."

Stefano shot to his feet, incredulous. "Shock doesn't describe it, *Papà*."

"Hear me out."

Stefano groaned and walked over to the mullioned windows looking out on the palatial estate with the snow-covered peaks of the Alps in the distance. An icy shiver passed through his taut body.

"Our two countries need to solidify in order to build the resources of both our kingdoms. This necessary merger can only happen by your marrying Princess Lanza."

Stefano wheeled around, gritting his teeth. "Years ago you gave me my freedom by parliamentary decree. I'm no longer a royal."

"That decree can be reversed by an emergency parliamentary edict."

"What?"

His father nodded. "I've already been investigating behind the scenes. Because of the enormity of this tragedy and their eagerness to see a marriage between our two countries happen, my advisors have informed me the parliament will reinstate you immediately."

Stefano couldn't believe it. "Even if it were possible, you're not seriously asking me to marry Princess Lanza, are you? I haven't been around her since she was a young girl. And I'm seven years older than she is."

"That's not a great age difference."

Stefano tried to calm down. "Alberto was the one who was attracted to her. I can't do this, *Papà*. Right now I'm doing everything in my power to develop more lucrative gold mines and invest the revenues to help our country grow richer. We don't need the timber from Domodossola!"

His father shook his head. "What I'm asking goes a great deal deeper than cementing fortunes. Victor and I have had this dream of uniting our two families in marriage since the moment we both became parents of future kings and queens."

"But it's not *my* dream, *Papà*, and never could be," Stefano said, attempting to control his anger. "I'm sorry, but I can't do what you ask."

"Not even to honor your brother?"

He hadn't realized his mother had come into the lounge wearing her dressing gown. The edge in her tone caught him off guard. "What do you mean, *Mamà*?"

"This has to do with keeping faith with a

sacred pledge your brother made to Princess Lanza a year ago. She's been groomed to become Alberto's bride. For the past year her life has been put on hold because she wears our family betrothal ring. All this time she's been faithful to their pledge, preparing for their wedding day."

Stefano shook his head. "No one could have imagined this crisis. It changes all the rules."

"Except for one thing your father and I have never told you about because we didn't think we would have to."

Fearing what he'd hear, Stefano's heart jolted in his chest. "What do you mean?"

"On the morning you turned eighteen, your brother came to us in secret. He wanted to give you a gift he knew you wanted more than anything on earth."

His brows furrowed. "What was that?"

"What else? Your freedom."

"I don't understand, *Mamà*."

"Then let me explain. You never wanted to be a royal. You made it clear from the time you were old enough to express your feelings. Alberto adored and worshipped you. By the time you turned eighteen, he was afraid you'd never be happy. He literally begged us to let you live a life free of royal duty.

"He loved you so much, he promised that he would fulfill all the things we would have asked of you as a royal prince who would rule one day so *you* could have the freedom to live life without the royal trappings. That was the bargain he made with us."

"A bargain? *That's* why you suddenly gave in to me?"

His father nodded solemnly. "The only reason, *figlio mio.* You two were so close, he put you before his own wants or desires. He convinced us you had to be able to go out in the world free to be your own person. Otherwise you'd die like an animal kept in a cage."

Alberto had actually told them that?

"All he asked was that we agree. Then he would do everything and more than we expected of him as a crown prince, *and*…he consented to become betrothed to Princess Lanza on whatever date we chose. He knew how much we loved her growing up. She was always a delight. In truth, he wanted his elder brother's happiness above all else, and made that request of us out of pure love."

Stefano stood there rigid as a piece of petrified wood. His parents had never lied to him. He had to believe them now. Because of his brother's love and intervention—and *not* because of his parents' understanding—Stefano had been able to escape the world he'd been born into all this time.

His mother walked over to him and put her hands on his shoulders. It pained him to see the lines of grief carved in her features.

"His only desire was that you never know how he pled for you. He worried that if you ever found out the truth, you would always feel beholden to him. That request was his unselfish gift to you."

Unselfish didn't begin to describe what Alberto had done to ensure his happiness.

In Stefano's mind and heart, it was an unheard-of gift. He'd always loved his younger brother, his buddy in childhood. Alberto's noble character made him beloved and elevated him above the ranks of ordinary people. Many times he'd heard people say that the good ones died young. His brother was the best of the best, and death had snatched him away prematurely.

Overcome with emotions assailing him, Stefano wrapped his arms around his mother until he could get a grip on them, then he let her go. He was amazed his parents had so much love for their sons that they'd gone along with both his and Alberto's wishes at the time. It was humbling and gave him new perspective.

Her eyes clung to his. "Would you be willing to do what Alberto can't do now? Take on the royal duty you were born to and marry Princess Lanza?"

He inhaled sharply. "Do you think she would consent when she'd planned to marry Alberto?"

"King Victor says his daughter will agree. You and Lanza knew each other in your youth and you have a whole year to get re-acquainted."

"But that will be close to impossible, *Papà.* My schedule has been laid out with back-to-back visits of all the mines through the next eighteen months. There's no time when so many managers are depending on me, especially with the new mining process I've developed."

His father cocked his head. "After we inform her and her parents of your official proposal of marriage, surely you could find a way to visit her once and stay in touch with her the rest of the time? Both King Victor and I have already talked to the cardinal, who has given this marriage his blessing."

Stefano could see the die had been cast.

His mother eyed him through drenched eyes. "Our two countries have been looking forward to this day since you were all children. The citizens know that your business interests throughout the world have contributed to our country's economy. Umbriano will cheer your reinstatement and honor your name for stepping into your brother's shoes, believe me."

Stefano found all this difficult to fathom. There wasn't time for him to get reacquainted with Princess Lanza. Even if parliament voted to reinstate him as a royal, he had crucial business issues around the globe.

His father walked over to them. "I've never asked anything of you before, Stefano. I've allowed you to be your own person, free of all royal responsibilities, but fate stepped in and took Alberto away too early. Now is the time when your parents and Lanza's are asking this for the good of both our countries."

"Alberto told us he hoped to have a family." His mother stared at him with longing. "I'm sure Princess Lanza was planning on children, too. That dream is gone, but you could make a whole new dream begin. I've had that dream for you, too, Stefano.

"On all your travels for business and pleasure, you've never brought a woman home for us to meet, let alone marry. We were prepared that you'd eventually want marriage and have a family, but it has never come to pass. If there's a special woman, you haven't said anything."

Stefano sucked in his breath. This whole conversation was unreal, including a discussion of a woman in his life he couldn't do without. He'd met several and had enjoyed some intimate relationships, but the thought of settling down with one of them hadn't entered his mind. As Alberto had said, he liked his freedom too much.

"Have you even considered Princess Lanza's feelings?" he asked them in a grating voice, struggling to make sense of this situation.

His father nodded. "King Victor and I talked about it before the funeral. He's as anxious as I for this to happen and has probably discussed this with her already. Victor assures me it's in her nature to do what is good for both countries."

No normal woman worth her salt would agree to such a loveless marriage, but a royal princess was a different matter if she believed it was her duty. Over the phone a few months ago, Alberto had told him in private that Princess Lanza had a sweet, biddable disposition.

Maybe she did. But the many royal princesses he'd met in his early teens were very spoiled, full of themselves, impossible to please, moody and felt entitled to the point of absurdity.

His vague memory of Lanza was that she was nice, but that was years ago and she'd been so young. His brother was a kind, decent human being. Alberto always tried to find the best in everyone and had probably made up his mind to like her.

After hearing what his parents had just told him about the sacrifice he'd made for Stefano, it was possible Alberto hadn't liked Princess Lanza at all. But he would have pretended otherwise to fulfill his obligations after making the incredible bargain with their parents. It was Alberto's way.

Stefano shook his head. He wasn't born with that kind of greatness in his soul. Humbled by what he'd learned, tortured by the decision his parents were asking him to make, he started for the door. "I need to be alone to think and will be back later."

Once outside in the chilling air, he drove his Lancia into the city to talk to his best friend, Enzo Perino, who managed his own father's banking interests. Stefano found him in his office on the phone.

The second Enzo saw him in the doorway, he waved him inside. After he hung up, he lunged from the chair to hug him. "I'm so sorry about Alberto."

"So am I, Enzo."

"Chiara and I couldn't get near you at the funeral. There were too many people." Stefano nodded. "Come to our house tonight for dinner so we can really talk."

He stared at his best friend who'd recently

married. They'd been friends throughout childhood and had done everything together, including military service. Stefano had been the best man at their wedding three months ago.

"I need help."

Enzo chuckled. "Since when have you ever needed a loan?"

Stefano sat down in one of the leather chairs. "I wish money were the problem, but it isn't."

As Stefano's father had emphasized, this suggested marriage had a lot more riding on it than financial considerations.

"You sound serious."

"More serious than you'll ever know."

"Go ahead. I'm listening."

"My father woke me up at the crack of dawn to have a talk." In the next few minutes he told Enzo the thrust of the conversation with his parents, including the necessary part about being reinstated by parliament.

"Our marriage will make me heir apparent to the throne of Domodossola since King Victor has no sons. He doesn't have any married daughters yet. According to their rules of succession, a woman can't become queen in their country. He'll have to rely on a son-in-law."

His friend whistled and sank down in the chair behind his desk. "I know this used to happen in the Middle Ages, but not today." He looked gutted. "Who will take over Umbriano when *your* father can no longer rule?"

"My sister, but I imagine that's many years away. Our country doesn't run by the same laws. You know that. Since I was granted my freedom, she's been raised to be second in line should anything happen to Alberto. Which it did," he said in a mournful tone.

"But if you're reinstated—"

"No—" He interrupted him. "My destiny lies with the throne of Domodossola, the only reason for reinstating me."

Enzo slapped his hands on the desk. "There goes the end of our friendship."

"Don't you ever say that!"

He smiled sadly. "How can I not? With you living in Domodossola, you'll be a prisoner running the affairs of government, hardly ever free to leave the country or have time for me. What will you do with all your mining companies?"

"I still plan to run them, of course."

"Then you'll be carrying a double load. I thought it was too good to be true when your father released you from your princely duties on your eighteenth birthday. We should have known it would all come to an early end."

Stefano closed his eyes for a minute, never imagining he'd lose his brother so young. "I haven't told my parents what I'm going to do. Not yet."

While he'd driven into town, he'd considered the huge decision his parents had made to give Stefano his freedom. In searching his soul, one thing became clear. He could solve his parents' dilemma about the marriage situation by unselfishly taking Alberto's place. How could he not when his brother had willingly done his double royal duty to make up for Stefano's absence?

"It'll happen," Enzo muttered. "I know how much you loved Alberto. You'll never let your parents down now that you know of your brother's sacrifice. As for Princess Lanza, she'll agree to marry you. After all, you are Alberto's brother and she knew you when your families got together as children."

"That's true, but I was hoping for some much-needed advice from you."

They stared at each other for a long time. "All right—there's only one way I can see this working. You need your freedom, so do her the biggest favor of her life and yours. You've got a year before the wedding. Let her know *before* you're married that you plan to be your own person and continue doing the mining work you love while you help her father govern. It'll mean you'll be apart from her for long periods. Give her time to adjust to that fact, know what I mean?"

* * *

Pain wasn't the right word to describe Lanza's feelings since returning from the funeral in Umbriano four days ago. Shock would be more precise. Prince Alberto had always been kind to her when they had met. She'd never felt uncomfortable with him.

The second-born son of her father's best friend, King Basilio of Umbriano, had been mild-mannered. Over the years and occasional family get-togethers, both families felt their two children were the perfect fit. Since they'd wanted the marriage to happen, they went ahead with the betrothal on her twenty-first birthday.

According to what her parents had told her, they'd believed that out of her two sisters, Lanza had the right temperament and disposition to be the wife for Prince Alberto, who'd shown an interest in her.

From that time on Lanza had spent several weekends a month with Alberto, both in Domodossola and Umbriano. They'd developed a friendship that helped her to get ready for her marriage. She'd enjoyed being kissed by him, but they hadn't been lovers.

The fact that he was nice-looking had made it easier to imagine intimacy in their marriage. She'd liked him well enough and believed they could be happy. But now that he was gone, one truth stood out from everything else.

She hadn't lost the love of her life.

Furthermore, his death had made her aware of her own singlehood in a way she would never have anticipated. Since the betrothal she'd known what her future would be. For the past year she'd been planning on the intimacy of marriage and family, the kind her parents enjoyed. Yet in an instant, that future had died with him.

His life had been snuffed out in seconds because of a car crash on an icy, narrow mountain road when he'd swerved to avoid a truck. The accident had robbed her of the destiny planned out for her. But as sorry as she was for Alberto and his family, a part of her realized that she was now free to make different plans.

There was no law of succession in Domodossola since a female couldn't rule. Now her parents would have to look elsewhere for a prince who would marry one of her older sisters, either Fausta or Donetta.

The sad, legitimate release of her betrothal vows gave Lanza a sense of liberation she'd never known before. Heaven help her but the thought was exciting. So exciting, in fact, she was assailed with uncomfortable guilt considering this was a time of mourning, and she *did* mourn Alberto's death.

In an attempt to help her deal with the fact that Prince Alberto had been taken prematurely, the palace priest, Father Mario, had been summoned. He counseled her that she should be grateful Alberto hadn't been forced to live through years of suffering. If his life had been spared, he might have lost limbs or been paralyzed.

Of course she was thankful for that and appreciated the priest's coming to see her, but no one understood what was going on inside her. No longer would she be marking time, waiting for her future with Alberto to start. There was no future except the one she would make from here on out. In truth, Lanza found the thought rich with possibilities.

Since returning from the funeral, it hit her with stunning force that she was alone and dependent on herself to make her own decisions, just like her sisters had been allowed to do. This strange new experience wasn't unlike watching a balloon that had escaped a string and was left to float with no direction in mind. But she knew what she wanted to do first.

With this new sense of freedom, she planned to visit her favorite aunt, Zia Ottavia, who lived in Rome with her husband, Count Verrini. They could talk about anything and Lanza loved her.

A knock on the door of her apartment brought her back from her thoughts.

"Lanza?" Her mother's voice. "May your father and I come in?"

She assumed they wanted to comfort her and she loved them for it. Lanza hurried across the room and opened the door, giving them both a long hug. "Come in and sit in front of the fire."

They took their places on the couch. She sat in her favorite easy chair across from them where she often planted herself to read. She'd been a bookworm from an early age.

"We asked Father Mario to visit you. Did he come?"

"Yes, and he gave me encouragement."

"Oh, good," her dark-blonde mother murmured, but Lanza could tell her parents were more anxious than ever and looked positively ill from the shock they'd all lived through. "We don't think it's good for you to stay in your apartment any longer. I've asked the cook to prepare your favorite meal, and your sisters are going to join us in the dining room for an early dinner."

Her distinguished-looking father nodded. "You need to be around family. It isn't healthy for you to be alone."

"Actually, I've needed this time to myself in order to think. Please don't be offended if I tell you I'm not hungry and couldn't eat a big meal."

"But if you keep this up, you'll waste away," her mother protested.

"No, *Mamà.* I promise that won't happen. Right now I have important things on my mind."

"We do, too," her father broke in. "It's time we talked seriously."

She sat back. "What is it, *Papà?*"

He got to his feet and stoked the fire. "I've been on the phone with Basilio almost constantly for days."

"That doesn't surprise me. I'm sure Alberto's death has brought you two even closer. He and Queen Diania must be in desperate need of comfort."

Her father blinked. "You're really not all right, are you, my dear girl?"

She frowned. "What do you mean?"

"You...don't seem quite yourself," her mother blurted.

If Lanza's parents had expected her to fall apart and take to her bed, then they truly didn't understand.

"I've shed my tears, but all it has done is give me a headache. I have to pull myself together and deal with the here and now. Honestly, I'll be fine. In fact, I'm thinking of taking a trip to Rome to visit Zia Ottavia.

"She phoned me last night and asked me to stay with her for a few months. She's planning to take a long trip to the US and wants me to go with her while Zio Salvatore has to stay in Rome on business. I love being with her and told her I'd come after I talked to you."

He shook his head. "I'm afraid you can't go."

What? She sat forward. "I don't understand."

He cleared his throat. "Alberto's brother, Stefano, has asked for your hand in marriage and wishes to marry you on New Year's Day in a year as planned."

CHAPTER TWO

A STRANGE LAUGH broke from Lanza, who got to her feet. Maybe she was having a bad dream.

"*Stefano?* What kind of a joke is this? For one thing, that's impossible! He was relieved of his royal duties years ago by their parliament."

Lanza had taken a personal affront to the news at the time, even though she knew it didn't have anything to do with her. How could it? She'd only been eleven years old.

But she still remembered how shocked she'd been when she'd heard Stefano had walked away from royal life. She'd always found him more attractive and headstrong than Alberto, but she'd never told anyone her true feelings.

Her father shook his head. "His royal title

has just been restored to him through an emergency act of that same parliament. Now he has officially proposed marriage to you."

Lanza let out a cry, incredulous that Stefano wanted to marry her when he'd hardly noticed her growing up. "Is it so important that our two countries combine our money and resources to the point that Stefano has been sent in to salvage the situation? He's the brother who wanted nothing to do with royal life!"

She knew she'd shocked her parents with an outburst that was totally unlike her. Never in her life had she dared speak her mind to them like this. But she felt frustrated and angry.

Her mother stood up and walked over to her. "We can understand your anger, darling, but please just listen. These have been dark days for all of us, but it's true that Stefano wants to take his brother's place and honor his commitment to you. It's what both our families want."

"But it's not what *I* want and I'm over

twenty-one!" Lanza stared at her parents in sheer disbelief. What they were asking went beyond rational thought. "You *do* know Stefano gave up the royal life years ago because he hated it."

"That's in the past," her father murmured.

"*Papà*—he's a gold-mining engineer and, according to Alberto, has had various love affairs with women where he's lived around the world. You're asking me to marry *him*? Are you serious?" she cried out.

Her mother's eyes implored her. "We're asking you to think about it and what it will mean for our two countries, for the future of both royal lines."

"I'm getting older every day," her father murmured. "Worse, I'm plagued by a fatigue that is growing more serious. I need a son-in-law to lean on who is fit to be king. Prince Stefano was raised like his brother, Alberto, and will make a splendid husband for you."

"But he's been a playboy!"

"No," her father argued. "What he has

done in his nonroyal past is what most men do before they find the right woman. There's been no scandal about him in the media. He's brought no shame of any kind. Quite the opposite. His brilliant business acumen is known around the world and has helped enrich his country. He's Basilio's son, after all."

"But Father—"

"Hear me out, Lanza. His private life before now has no bearing on the future. That part is over."

"How do you know he doesn't have children somewhere? I'm not trying to be cruel by saying that, only practical."

His expression hardened. "I'm going to forget you said that. He's prepared to be a husband to you."

Lanza was too stunned to talk. She studied her father, worried if it was true that he was ill. This was news no one had told her about. "Why haven't I heard about your health before now, *Papà*?" She'd noticed he moved a little slower these days, but she attributed it to his growing older.

Her mother put a hand on her arm. "Because we didn't want to burden you while you were preparing for your wedding day. We were assuming you wouldn't have to worry about it, but with Alberto dying, everything has changed. Under the circumstances we'll leave to give you time to think about everything." She turned to Lanza's father. "Come on, Victor."

As Lanza watched them go, her two older sisters came in and shut the door. She sucked in her breath. "I take it you could hear us talking."

They nodded.

"Is it true? Is *Papà* ill?"

"I only know what *Mamà* said." Donetta spoke first. "*Papà*'s physician is concerned about his health and says he needs to slow down."

Fausta nodded. "I have a feeling it's his heart, but they won't tell us."

Lanza shivered and walked over to the fireplace. "Why didn't you two tell me?"

Donetta drew closer. "We were ordered not to."

"In other words, I'm the baby who can't handle bad news."

"No. They've been living for your wedding and didn't want anything to mar it."

She closed her eyes tightly. "What they've asked me now is impossible, but I shouldn't have gotten so upset with them."

"Yes, you should have!" Fausta blurted. "I'm proud of you. You haven't seen Prince Stefano in years. Naturally, we're all worried that something is wrong with *Papà*, but even so, you shouldn't let this news make you do what you don't want to do."

Donetta nodded. "I hate to tell you this, Lanza, but you've always been a lot like Cinderella from your favorite fairy tale. She, too, was sweet and believed everything would turn out in the end. But you don't have a fairy godmother to save you. Otherwise, Alberto wouldn't have died. You need to wake up before it's too late."

"She's right!" Fausta chimed once more, adding to Lanza's turmoil. "Cinderella was a fool. She should have gone out into the world to find a man of the people, not some puppet prince, and enjoy a life away from a royal world. That's what I'm planning to do."

Lanza understood her sisters well. Twenty-five-year-old Donetta had no intention of getting married and her parents knew it. But the day would come when they would demand that she marry some prince they approved of.

She'd grown up wanting to be queen, with no man telling her what to do, but it would be impossible because of the succession law of their country that excluded women from ruling.

As for Fausta, their twenty-four-year-old sister, she'd dreamed of marrying a commoner and having a life like her close friends in the city. Fausta thought she was safe, but in the end their parents wouldn't allow it and she'd end up marrying a prince they'd picked out for her.

That left Lanza as her parents' hope for finding the perfect royal son-in-law. But Alberto's death had rendered that null and void. Or so she'd thought!

"We know how upset you are. Would you rather be alone?"

Lanza turned to Fausta. "If you don't mind, I've got a lot to think about."

"We'll eat dinner and then come back up to talk. We're here if you need us." Donetta gave her a peck on the cheek before they left the apartment.

Lanza turned toward the fire once more. What in the name of heaven was she going to do? She loved her father. The last thing she'd ever want would be to disappoint him or her mother, or do something that could make his condition worse.

But to be asked to marry Stefano, who'd turned his back on everything in order to be free…

She remembered one weekend in August when Alberto had come to see her and she'd asked him why he sometimes seemed sad. Lanza wanted to know the truth so she could understand him better.

Alberto told her he missed his elder brother terribly since he no longer lived at the palace. They'd been incredibly close. A few days later Alberto sent her a letter with a picture of Stefano enclosed, looking gorgeous in a safari shirt. He'd been twenty-two in the photo, taken when he'd been working in Kenya.

"I love that smile of his, Lanza. He's my idol and always has been. There are times when I miss him like crazy. After you and I are married, I hope he'll come around more often. I'd give anything to see more of him."

Lanza stoked the fire, recalling those words that had come straight from Alberto's heart. He'd gotten his wish far too late. Stefano was back, and had proposed marriage to *her*.

Stefano was an important, sophisticated

man of the world and had been intimately involved with various women over the years, according to the media, so there were no surprises. If Alberto had been with other women this past year, Lanza knew nothing about it, but assumed he'd had a few girlfriends in the past.

Marrying Stefano would mean having a normal intimate relationship that would produce a family in time. Her attraction for him had never changed, even though they hadn't seen one another for a long time, but for some reason the thought of having relations with him made her nervous. She was an inexperienced and naive virgin. A shudder passed through her body.

Would she be a disappointment as his wife?

Could she bring herself to accept another royal proposal of marriage?

If she did, it might increase her father's longevity and give him the help he needed to rule. She loved her father. Perish the thought if he died early because she'd refused to go through with this marriage. How would she be able to bear the burden of that knowledge?

Lanza was a mess.

Her sisters were right. Her favorite fairy tale *had* been about Cinderella, who'd met her heart's desire at the ball and had lived happily-ever-after with her prince. But that was never going to happen to her now.

When Lanza finally turned away from the fire, she accepted the fact that she'd been a fool her whole life…

I'll never know love or be in love.

On that note she left the apartment to find her parents and tell them she'd made her decision to accept Stefano's proposal, but was stopped on her way out the door by her personal maid.

"This came for you personally by courier from the royal palace in Umbriano, Your Highness."

"Thank you, Serena."

Lanza went back into the apartment to open it. Letters of condolences had poured into the palace for days through the post, but this had been hand delivered. There was no writing on the outside of the envelope. Who would be sending her a letter?

Curious, she opened it and found a brief missive.

Dear Lanza,

What you and I are about to do is unprecedented. I've already had to leave the country for Kenya, where I'll probably be working for at least six weeks. After that I must fly directly to Australia, and from there Bulgaria.

I'll try to get to Domodossola at some point to see you. If I can't, I'll email you so we can talk regularly and get prepared for the wedding. Phone calls are difficult because the mines where I work rarely have cell phone service.

I'm afraid our life will have to begin after we meet at the altar.

Don't worry about our wedding night.

*We'll spend it away from everyone while
we sort out the rules of engagement.
Stefano*

She gasped in surprise. Before she'd even
given her parents or him her answer, Stefano had already sent this message assuming she would have fallen in line with their
parents' wishes.

What on earth did he mean about the rules
of engagement, unless he was implying he
had a solution they could live with?

Lanza sank down on the side of the bed,
confused and unsettled as she reread it. Stefano's work truly did take him around the
world. When would he have time to help
her father? Maybe she shouldn't marry him,
after all.

"Lanza?"

"Just a minute." Hearing her sisters'
voices, she quickly buried the letter beneath
a cushion on her bed and hurried over to the
door to open it. "Come on in."

"We thought you might want company."

She didn't know what she wanted.

"Have you decided what you're going to do?"

"Not yet. *Papà* said this marriage has the blessing of the cardinal. He says the citizens of both countries will accept it. But I think it seems like a sham and I feel guilty about it. Do you think it sounds honorable for Stefano to take Alberto's place?"

Fausta eyed her with concern. "It's a year away, and they were close. I do remember that."

"But I don't love him."

"Did you love Alberto?"

She lowered her head. "No, but I liked him well enough. If I say yes and agree to marry Stefano, it will be because *Papà* needs a son-in-law to rely on."

"No." Donetta came back with a friendly smile. "That won't be the reason. You can't fool Fausta and me."

"What do you mean?"

"We both know you always had a crush

on Stefano. Who could blame you? As the tabloids say, he's the dishiest bachelor on the planet."

CHAPTER THREE

One year later...

A WINTRY NEW YEAR'S DAY brought thousands of people to line the streets of the capital of Domodossola for the royal wedding. A national holiday had been declared and the sound of bells rang out.

The kingdom had been preparing for this event since her betrothal to Alberto two years ago. Now that day was finally here with a different prince walking her down the aisle. Every shop was open to welcome visitors from all over Europe and beyond.

Lanza sat across from her father in the gold leaf closed carriage that took them toward the cathedral in the distance. With every step of the matched white horses in trappings of red and gold bells that jingled, huge cheers from the masses rang out to celebrate this day unlike any other. Excitement filled the air to see the king accompanying his daughter to the long-anticipated wedding ceremony.

Over the year she'd received dozens of long emails with pictures from Stefano while they'd discussed the plans for the wedding in the cathedral and the festivities afterward at the palace.

She'd asked him questions about his locations and work. He'd explained a lot of technical things about mining she'd enjoyed. His descriptions of the people and mountains painted pictures that lived with her. Lanza hadn't counted on him being such a satisfying letter writer, and she'd found herself eagerly looking forward to reading them when they came.

But they hadn't touched on their personal, intimate relationship yet. She was still anxious to talk to him about the *rules of engagement*. Those words had been dancing around in her head since his letter had arrived close to a year ago.

What had Stefano really meant? If only he'd explained, it might have helped her get through this ordeal without so much angst. Those words had sounded cold and unfeeling coming from a worldly man who'd managed to avoid a royal life until now. Now that they were about to exchange vows, her fraught nerves had made her too jumpy to concentrate on anything.

What she'd give to get out of the carriage and run for her life. Then she glanced at her father with his salt-and-pepper hair, who looked splendid despite the fact that he did move slower these days. The love in his eyes when he smiled at her helped her remember one of the reasons why she was going through with this farce of a marriage.

Her father had been living for this day for years and might be granted a longer life because she'd agreed to marry his best friend's only son now that Alberto was gone.

"You look so beautiful in all that silk and lace, my angel daughter."

"Thank you, *Papà*, but I'm not your angel." He'd always called her that, but since the day she'd learned her parents expected her to marry Stefano, she hadn't felt very angelic.

Through her mother, who talked constantly with Stefano's mother, Lanza had learned Stefano planned to whisk her away for a two-week honeymoon to a secret spot in the Caribbean. She now had a wardrobe of beachwear.

Two weeks alone in paradise.

"I'm going to miss you around the palace while you're on your honeymoon, my sweet girl."

She wasn't as sweet as her father thought. "I'll miss you, too. Today you look magnificent, like the king you are. I love you and I'm sorry abou—"

"Let's not talk about that day," he interrupted. "We were all beside ourselves. You've brought me joy your whole life and it's all in the past. Promise me you'll forget it."

Her eyes smarted. "If you can, then I will, too."

But she would never forget. By agreeing to marry Stefano, all hope for personal happiness had died. Her mind kept going back to the note he'd had couriered to her.

They were definitely doing something unprecedented.

Soon the closed carriage drew up in front of the steps of the fourteenth-century cathedral. One of the footmen opened the door. She held her bouquet of white roses and stephanotis as he helped her step out, giving the press an opportunity to see her in all her wedding finery and take pictures.

Her chestnut-colored hair had been swept back and cascaded beyond her shoulders. The lace veil draped over the pearl tiara worn by her great-great-grandmother fell to her chin in front and flowed down her back to meet the hem of her gown with its long train.

Her father got out behind her and accompanied her up the steps to the roar and cheers of the thousands of people filling the streets. Lanza's mother and sisters, along with her aunts, uncles and cousins, had already gone inside with the other dignitaries and waited in the pews. By now Prince Stefano's entire family from Umbriano, including their future queen and her young children, would have already entered and been seated.

Once inside the doors, Lanza heard the glorious organ music and choir, catching her off guard. She took a deep breath, realizing the moment had come when she had to pledge her life to a man who'd lost a brother, hated royal life and was as unhappy as Lanza.

The wedding march sounded, alerting her this was it. Her father turned to look at her. "Are you ready?"

No…

Like an automaton, she put her free hand on his left arm, and they walked into the Romanesque nave that was packed wall to wall with the invited guests turned out in elegant dress. The fascinators worn by the women made the scene resemble a garden even though it was winter.

With each step that took her closer to the altar where the cardinal stood resplendent in red and gold robes, her legs felt less substantial. Then she saw Stefano waiting in a magnificent royal suit of navy and gold braid. Across his chest from shoulder to waist he wore the bright blue sash of his office as Prince of the Realm of Umbriano.

At the funeral she'd hardly noticed him with everyone around. They'd all been in mourning. Lanza had been in such deep shock, she hadn't realized that over the years he'd grown taller than Alberto. Looking at him now, he probably stood six foot two and was built of rock-hard muscle.

A little closer and she gasped quietly. His burnished complexion reflected his work and travel in hot climates. Mesmerized, her gaze roved over his chiseled features set beneath dark brows and wavy black-brown hair. The boy had become a breathtaking man.

As the tabloids had claimed leading up to the marriage, he was a dashing male specimen. She suspected he had to shave twice a day and was more gorgeous than her idea of any prince in an old fairy tale.

Her heart tripped over itself. Stefano was going to be *her* husband. The man she would go to bed with and whose children she'd bear. She gripped her father's arm harder and continued walking until they reached the cardinal, who put out his arms.

"Come stand in front of me."

Stefano moved to Lanza's side. She let go of her father's arm and handed Donetta the flowers, then turned back to meet his dark, penetrating eyes. A thunderbolt passing through her body couldn't have been more electrifying. Shaken by emotions new to her and an instant awareness of him, she transferred her gaze to the cardinal, who opened with some prayers, before proceeding to the marriage ceremony.

"Stefano Amadeo Piero Casale, wilt thou have this woman to thy wedded wife, to live together according to God's law in the holy estate of matrimony? Wilt thou love her, comfort her, honor and keep her, in sickness and in health; and, forsaking all others, keep thee only unto her, so long as ye both shall live?"

"I will," he said in a deep voice Lanza felt resonate to her toes.

"Lanza Vittoria Immaculata Rossiano, wilt thou have this man to thy wedded husband, to live together according to God's law in the holy estate of matrimony? Wilt thou love him, comfort him, honor him, keep him, in sickness and in health; and, forsaking all others, keep thee only unto him, so long as ye both shall live?"

"I will."

"You will now exchange rings."

Stefano, not missing a heartbeat, reached for her left hand and slid a ring with the royal Umbriano crest on her finger. She in turn put the gold band with the Rossiano crest on his ring finger. She felt tense and wondered if he could tell. "In as much as Stefano and Lanza have consented together in holy wedlock, and have witnessed the same before God and this company, and thereto have given and pledged their troth either to other, and have declared the same by giving and receiving of a ring, and by joining of hands, I pronounce that they be man and wife together, in the name of the Father, and of the Son and of the Holy Ghost. Amen.

"You may kiss the bride, Your Highness."

A year ago Lanza had worn the black veil of mourning. Since then Stefano had been imagining this moment. When she'd approached him at the altar—a vision in white silk—her white lace veil had given him enticing glimpses of her lovely features and deep blue eyes. As he lifted it, what he hadn't counted on was her true classic beauty or the voluptuous shape of her mouth.

His heart pounded hard as he lowered his head to kiss her. Much as he wanted to taste her fully, he held back and only brushed his mouth against hers. The soft sweetness of her lips sent a sensation not unlike electricity through his body. The princess he'd met when she was just a young girl had grown into a breathtaking woman who was now his wife. *His wife!*

"We'll talk in the carriage," he whispered against the fragrant silky skin of her cheek before he lifted his head.

Organ music filled the cathedral while he took her hand in a firm grip. Donetta came forward to give her the flowers and they started down the aisle. He was now a married man who'd made promises to his new bride, who walked at his side. They made their way outside to the ringing of the cathedral bells, followed by bells ringing out all over the city.

He felt like they were part of a dream as he helped her into the same carriage he knew she'd ridden in with her father. Stefano climbed in and sat opposite her, hoping she'd meet his eyes. "This is where we have to wave at the crowd. They're eager to see the beautiful princess and take pictures."

"If the temperature keeps falling, maybe everyone will go home."

He studied her features. "You know they won't. This wedding has been anticipated for two years."

She nodded. "We're part of the fairy tale meant to be exciting for them, but by midnight it'll all be over and the real test of living will begin."

Stefano sat back. "I am guessing from that comment you received the message I sent you when we got engaged. But in all our emails, you never mentioned it."

She continued waving. "I'm sorry that I didn't. If you want to know the truth, it was like a breath of fresh air."

One dark brow lifted. "Why do you say that?"

"You indicated that there are ways to negotiate our situation. It gave me hope that you have something brilliant in mind. Alberto said you were born with the real brains in the family."

So saying, she turned to the windows on the other side of the carriage. For the next little while she fulfilled her part in acknowledging the crowds cheering and taking pictures.

They weren't really going to have a chance to talk properly today; that would have to wait till they left to go on their honeymoon. That time couldn't come soon enough for Stefano. He didn't want their marriage to start off with this kind of tension.

"Uh-oh!" she exclaimed. "Don't stop waving, *Signor* Casale. Alberto told me that's the name you go by at your many gold mines throughout the world. Time's not up yet. We only have to endure this display for the masses for a few more minutes."

The woman who'd sent him enchanting emails he'd thoroughly enjoyed was not in evidence right now. Soon the carriage arrived back at the fifteenth-century palace. She faced him with a smile. "All we must do now is endure this endless day a little longer."

The footman opened the door of the carriage, but Stefano got out first to help her. No matter her true feelings, whatever they were, he was determined to behave in every way like an adoring bridegroom, even arranging her veil and train. With her flowers in one hand, he grasped her other hand and they ascended the steps past the palace staff who'd assembled to welcome them.

He walked her through the rotunda where their families awaited them. After many hugs, she turned to him. "I'm going down the hall to freshen up, but I'll be back."

"Would you like me to go with you?"

"Thank you, but I won't be long."

"Then I'll wait right here for you."

"You don't have to."

His eyes searched hers. "Don't you know I want to?"

CHAPTER FOUR

STEFANO HAD SOUNDED like he'd meant it. Lanza went to the waiting room more confused over her feelings about him than ever before returning to the rotunda. He saw her coming and walked toward her.

"Are you all right?"

"Of course. Why do you ask?"

"You look a little pale."

"I'll be fine when I eat."

He cupped her elbow, and they joined the guests in the enormous ballroom decorated for their wedding feast. According to her mother, no expense had been spared to make this the most lavish affair since her father had been crowned king.

They sat at the head table with their royal parents on either side of them. Stefano couldn't have been more accommodating, seeing to her every need as they ate. His behavior and noble bearing were impeccable.

The way he waited on her and was so attentive, she had the impression he'd convinced everyone this was a match made in heaven. She was bewildered because deep inside her she knew he hadn't wanted this marriage.

Her father gave the first toast. "To my new son-in-law, Stefano, who has made me and my wife the happiest people in Domodossola, except for our daughter. Her radiant countenance speaks for itself. To the bride and groom and a lifetime of joy!"

Everyone drank from their champagne glasses. Stefano touched his flute to hers with a smile. "I'm relieved to see more color in your cheeks."

"I didn't realize how hungry I was."

"Is there anything else I can get you?"

"No, thank you."

This should be the most exciting, thrilling night of her life, but Stefano didn't love her and she wasn't foolish enough to pretend otherwise.

At that point Stefano's father stood on his feet. "Victor took the words right out of my mouth. My wife and I are overjoyed. Over the years we've been delighted to anticipate the day when Princess Lanza would become our daughter-in-law. Now it is here. To Stefano and Lanza. We couldn't ask for a greater blessing."

Again, Stefano touched her glass with his and they sipped their champagne. Then to her surprise, he stood up. Looking down at her he said, "Lanza? Will you stand up with me?"

After she got to her feet, he slid his arm beneath her veil to get it around her waist and pulled her next to him. "I'm the luckiest of men today. There's no bride to compare to her. Wouldn't you all agree?" His comment produced cheers and clapping.

Warmth filled her cheeks. When she looked at her sisters sitting next to her mother and father, she knew what to say in response. "With three daughters, my parents have waited a long time for a son. Who better than the son of my father's best friend, a man he reveres?"

Then everyone got to their feet for one more toast. King Basilio sent her a special smile that seemed to come from his heart. Then everyone sat down.

She watched her father get up again. "The fireworks are starting. We'd like to invite everyone to go through the side doors of the ballroom to the balcony. Stefano? If you and Lanza will lead the way. The crowds are waiting for you."

He helped her up, and they walked together. On their way out in the chilly night air he pulled her close again. "You made my father very happy just now."

"They're all happy," she murmured back. Without waiting for a response, she moved ahead of him to the balcony railing.

The sight of their winter wonderland kingdom waving and cheering at them from the lighted palatial estate came as another emotional moment, like the one when she'd stepped inside the cathedral and heard the magnificent music of the organ and choir. How sad their marriage was such a travesty of a proper wedding.

Stefano joined her and found her hand, holding it with enough strength that she couldn't shake it off. Of course she wouldn't have.

Before everyone got too cold, they went inside and cut the eight-tiered wedding cake. Her awareness of him was growing so strong, she could hardly eat any of it. Lanza despised her own weakness for being vulnerable to anything to do with him.

His dark gaze found hers. "Our bags have already been taken out to the limo. We need to leave soon to make our flight. I'll meet you in the rotunda in a half hour."

"Maybe that's possible for you. But it's obvious you've never had to get yourself out of a wedding dress with thirty tiny buttons holding it up. My sisters will do their best."

She nodded to Donetta and Fausta, who

left their parents to accompany her out of the ballroom to her suite on the second floor of the palace. On the bed, Serena had laid out the designer eggshell-colored two-piece suit with lace on the hems of the sleeves.

After they helped Lanza remove the veil and tiara, they turned her around. "How do you feel now?" Fausta wanted to know as she worked on the bottom half of buttons. Donetta stood on her other side to undo the top ones.

"I'm so exhausted, I have no idea how I feel. Tomorrow when I'm lying on a beach, I'll be better able to tell you."

"Good grief, he's handsome!"

"You can say that again," Donetta commented. "The women must be crazy about him."

Fausta nodded. "But he's out of circulation now."

"One can hope."

"Oh, Donetta, what a thing to say."

Lanza didn't like hearing any of it and stepped out of her gown. She didn't want to believe Donetta's teasing comment. He was her husband now. "Thanks for helping me."

Wanting to avoid talk, she gathered up her new underwear and hurried into the bathroom for a quick shower. Afterward, she swept her hair back on her head and secured it with a pearl comb. It matched her pearl earrings and the single pearl on a gold chain Stefano had sent her ahead of time as a wedding gift.

She fastened it around her neck, touched up her lipstick, then came back out to dress in the suit. Once she'd put on her high heels, she slipped on the new beige cashmere coat that fell above the knee and tied with a sash at the waist.

Her gaze flew to the clock by her bed. She'd already been gone an hour. Lanza reached for the cream-colored leather handbag and kissed her sisters.

"You look beautiful," they both said at the same time.

"Thank you. See you in two weeks."

They caught up to her at the door. Donetta

eyed her with concern. Fausta looked just as worried. "Are you all right?"

She stared at them, deciding to be honest. "No, and I'm not sure I ever will be again, but you two already know that. I won't be throwing the bouquet, and you both know why." Donetta didn't want to get married. One day Fausta would find her man of the people, but unfortunately their parents could intervene and turn their wishes around.

Lanza blew them another kiss and hurried through the palace and down the stairs. The girls, uncharacteristically quiet, followed her.

Stefano stood out from everyone at the bottom of the elegant staircase beneath the rotunda. Her striking new husband had changed into an elegant dark gray suit, shirt and tie, reminding her of a highly successful, sophisticated CEO. He wore an overcoat close to the color of hers and was surrounded by their families, who were waiting to wave them off.

"Here she comes," her mother said as both

her parents rushed toward her and gave her a hug. "You look perfectly lovely, darling."

"Thanks, *Mamà*."

"You'll never know how happy we are for you," her father murmured.

He was wrong. She knew exactly how they felt, but her dad looked weary tonight. It had been such a long day. Lanza had to pray that if nothing else came of it, this marriage would add a few years to his life.

She hugged him extra hard. "Relax and enjoy this time now that the wedding is over, *Papà*. We'll be back before you know it."

"Lanza?"

She let go of her father and walked over to him. "Yes, *Signor* Casale?" she said in a quiet aside. When she saw his slight grimace, it brought a smile to her face.

He put his arm through hers and they left the palace in the biting cold for the limo waiting below. After they got inside and the chauffeur drove them around the drive to the road in the distance, Stefano turned to her.

"I'm curious to know the real reason why

you insist on calling me *Signor* Casale." He sat next to her rather than opposite her like they'd done in the carriage.

"I'm sorry and won't do it again. One of my favorite novels is *Pride and Prejudice*. In the story, the mother of the four Bennett daughters always speaks to her husband as Mr. Bennett. She never uses his first name, never calls him honey or darling or sweetheart or dearest. She's absolutely hilarious and I laugh every time."

"You read it often?" He wasn't able to hide his surprise.

"I've read it a lot in my life. Are you a reader?"

"When I have time."

"What's one of your favorite novels?"

"I'll have to think about that."

She let the comment go and crossed her legs at the ankles. "While we're alone, let me thank you for the lovely necklace you sent me. I'm wearing it now."

"I noticed. It's made from the gold of one of our mines in Umbriano."

"That was very thoughtful. I'll treasure it. What about the pearl?"

"I purchased it in Japan a long time ago." It looked like a pregnant pear.

"I can always replace it with something you would like better, perhaps a diamond?"

"Don't you dare." She touched it with her fingers. "I'm sure there's not another pearl like this one in existence." Actually, she loved its unique shape.

She had a gift for him, but it was packed in her luggage.

Before long they reached the airport and were driven to the area where the private planes landed. In a minute they arrived outside the royal jet with the King of Umbriano's insignia.

The steward came down the steps of the jet and loaded their luggage. Stefano got out of the limo to help Lanza. Cupping her elbow, he walked up the steps with her into the luxurious interior and introduced her.

"My name is Corso. I'm honored to meet you, Your Highness. It's a privilege."

"I'm very happy to meet you."

Stefano led her to the club compartment and helped her off with her coat.

She felt those dark, probing eyes rove over her as she sat down and fastened her seat belt.

"You look stunning in that suit."

Lanza wondered how many women he'd said that to in the past, but she needed to stop thinking about what had gone on before. The last thing she wanted to act like was a jealous wife.

"Your gift gave it the touch it needed."

The engines fired and she saw the fasten seat belt sign flash. He sat across from her and buckled up. She knew he was anxious to get going. That was fine with her, but Lanza couldn't imagine anything more nerve-racking than going to a beach with him. She barely knew him, and part of her wished this was a bad dream and she'd wake up to find herself alone.

"If you'd like something to eat or drink, I'll tell Corso."

"Nothing for me, but thank you."

Exhausted after such a long day, she closed her eyes, anxious to fall asleep and avoid the inevitable small talk neither of them had any desire to engage in. By the time she awakened, they would have landed somewhere in the Caribbean.

But it seemed like she'd barely dropped off when she heard the ding of the fasten seat belt sign and opened her eyes. They couldn't possibly have been in the air very long. She could feel increasing turbulence. Lanza darted him a glance. "Do you know why we had to land?"

He eyed her intently. "Unbeknownst to our families, I changed our honeymoon destination and instructed the pilot to fly us to Umbriano."

The jet was starting to descend against strong winds. This part of the Alps was known for its fierce weather. "Apparently right into the heart of winter," she drawled. "This must be why you told me to hurry."

"I heard a storm front was moving in fast."

"I presume you had no taste for a beach honeymoon, either, but our families will continue to fantasize. This is *their* wedding day, after all, the one they've dreamed of since we were children."

She undid her seat belt, but before she could get up, Corso came in carrying a pair of women's leather lace-up boots he handed to Stefano.

Her husband had already gotten to his feet and put on his overcoat. "You'll need to remove your high heels so they won't get ruined in the snow."

"Thank you. You've managed to think of everything." As soon as she'd taken them off, he put them inside his coat pockets. The man was full of surprises.

While she tied the boots, Corso took their luggage out of the plane. Stefano helped her into her coat and together they walked to the entrance and down the steps. Snow had been falling, spattered by the wind.

An attractive man with blue eyes and dark blond hair she'd met at the wedding reception stood outside an all-terrain vehicle. Right now he was wearing a ski hat and parka. The steward loaded their bags at the back.

Stefano turned to her. "Lanza? You remember my very best friend, Enzo Perino."

"Of course." They shook hands.

His eyes played over her features in male admiration. "I couldn't be more honored, Your Highness. You were a vision today when you walked down the aisle in the cathedral with your father. Stefano is the luckiest of men."

Hardly… But for some reason she liked his friend on sight.

"Thank you, Enzo. Please call me Lanza."

He flashed Stefano a smile before opening the rear door for them. "You're going to freeze to death if you don't get in where it's warm."

How funny. Other than her coat, she hadn't brought a stitch of winter clothing with her.

Stefano followed her inside and shut the door. It felt good to get out of the freezing wind. He helped her find the seat belt so she could fasten it. Every time he brushed against her, she smelled the scent of the soap he'd used in the shower and she was increasingly aware of his potent male aura. Her attraction to him was blinding her to the pragmatic reason why they'd married.

Enzo got behind the wheel. Before starting out, he said, "I'm very aware of my precious cargo and will drive as safely as I can."

That was a very thoughtful thing for him to say considering Alberto had been killed on a winter road.

They headed out of the airport. Obviously, their flight had landed just in time. Snow had started falling and pelted the windshield. They'd barely made it here ahead of the storm.

She assumed they were headed for a hotel, but she couldn't have been more wrong when she saw the turnoff he'd taken for the mountains.

"Where are we going?" she asked in a quiet aside.

"Home to my chalet. We'll be there within forty-five minutes."

"So you had a home here when you returned to Umbriano after your various trips?"

"For the last ten years, yes."

"That's one secret not leaked to the public. It means you were given your own hideaway at eighteen along with your freedom." Every young prince dying to be released from the royal trappings should be so blessed.

"Actually, I purchased it with my own earnings."

Lanza swallowed hard at her unintentional gaffe. "Did Alberto envy you?"

She had to wait for his answer. "Alberto loved it as much as I did. My wedding present to him was that he bring you to the chalet for your honeymoon after you were married. It was going to be a secret from everyone else."

His response was so unexpected and touching, she could hardly breathe. Alberto had been planning to bring her to Stefano's hideaway in the mountains?

Lanza wished she hadn't brought up his brother's name while he was still grieving.

Unsettled, she leaned forward. "Enzo? Did you spend time at the chalet with Stefano when you two were young?"

"All the time. We skied, mountain climbed, hunted, fished, camped out and had parties."

"I'll bet. Sounds like heaven."

"But as we got older we haven't had as much time to do that as we've been busy pursuing our careers."

"What kind of work do you do?"

"I went to university and got my degree in finance. Since then I've worked in my father's bank. Lately I've taken over more and more of his duties because his health is failing."

"How wonderful for him to have a son like you."

Stefano would be doing the same thing for her father. *But not Stefano's own father...*

Though she knew his sister would be queen one day, she wondered how King Basilio really felt about losing his firstborn son this way. Was Stefano conflicted, as well?

"It's very generous of you to drive us to the chalet this late, Enzo."

"After all the things Stefano has done for me in my life, I'll never be able to repay him." She heard real affection in his tone. Stefano remained quiet.

The snow continued relentlessly as they climbed in altitude to the higher peaks. Enzo was being very careful. Few cars were on the treacherous mountain road, the kind where Alberto had lost his life.

She sat back, growing more anxious because they'd be alone soon in his private home away from civilization.

Before long Enzo turned off the main road and drove along what seemed like a path lined with snow-swept pines winding for several miles. Eventually, he pulled up to a massive gate that swung open electronically. He drove on through and around to an alpine chalet whose roof was covered by at least two feet of snow, but she could barely see the outline.

Stefano got out to help her. She was glad he'd thought ahead and had brought her new boots to put on. The snow was deep. Under the fresh layer coming down lay more snow from other storms. Enzo took the bags from his car, and they entered Stefano's secret domain.

A light went on. The lower level housed everything; shovels, hunting gear, skis, snowshoes, camping gear, snowboards, a snow-shoveling machine, a generator, a freezer and a washer and dryer. Stefano could live here self-contained.

"Shall we go upstairs?"

Lanza followed him and Enzo to the next floor where several lamps went on. She was struck immediately by the light wood floors and rafters. On one wall she saw an enormous fireplace set behind glass, lending the vaulted room a chic yet rustic elegance. Stefano turned it on so the flames lit up the interior. Instant heat.

Attractive twin couches in a claret color faced each other in front of a low, large square coffee table with a colorful ceramic pot. It was probably from Mexico where she'd heard one of his gold mines was located.

On one wall stood a massive breakfront with books on two shelves. There were many small pictures of Stefano's family on a third shelf. The bottom one contained magazines and board games.

She turned around to view the floor-to-ceiling windows that would give a spectacular mountain outlook during the day. There was a refectory-style table and chairs off the kitchen with its wood cabinets and slate floors.

Enzo had disappeared down a hallway with their luggage. When he reappeared, he paused at the stairway. "I wish the two of you every happiness and a wonderful honeymoon. Now I've got to get back to my own wife."

"Thank you for everything, Enzo."

"My pleasure."

"Be careful going down the canyon. That's a heavy snow out there."

He smiled. "We're used to it, aren't we, Stefano?"

Her husband nodded. "I'll walk you out." Before he left the room, he turned to Lanza. "I'm sure you must be exhausted. Your bedroom is down the hall to the left. Just so you know, earlier this month I asked Carla to buy you some winter clothes. When I returned to Umbriano a few days ago, I put them in your closet."

"That was very thoughtful. Thank you."

He nodded. "If you're hungry or thirsty, make yourself at home in the kitchen. I have things to do so I'll see you in the morning and we'll talk then." The two men disappeared down the stairs.

In the letter Stefano had couriered to her a year ago, he'd warned Lanza there'd be no wedding night. She'd taken him at his word and there'd been no mention of it during their exchange of emails.

While they were gone, Lanza explored the rest of the chalet. There were two bedrooms with light wood floors, rugs and ensuite bathrooms. Her bags had been put in what was obviously a guest bedroom with a queen-size bed and dresser. A TV sat on top of it. She removed her coat and boots, putting them in the closet where she saw the winter clothes.

After finding a pair of flats in one of her cases, she put them on and decided to do the rest of her own unpacking in a little while.

Curious to see everything, she went across the hall. Stefano's bedroom showed signs of being permanently occupied with a cubby full of various winter wear. He had his own TV and radio. A mural that showed the Casale gold mines around the world took up one wall. She intended to study it, but not when he was around.

The desk on the other wall contained a

state-of-the-art computer and printer, led-gers, mining books, everything he needed for his work. His bags had been placed at the end of the king-size bed.

Afraid to be caught trespassing in his thor-oughly masculine domicile, she hurried back to the living room and wandered into the kitchen. The fridge appeared stocked with food and drinks. Over the past few days Stefano must have been busy getting all this ready.

She reached for a cola and walked back to the main room to examine some of the books. *The Thirty-Nine Steps* by John Bu-chan caught her attention. She wondered if Stefano had read it recently, or even read it at all. She took it to the bedroom with her and shut the door.

How bizarre to be alone with a strange man who'd only been her husband for about nine hours.

Needing to unwind, she opened her cases and unpacked the rest of her clothes. In one of the pockets she'd packed her wrapped gift for Stefano. She pulled it out and put it on the dresser to give him in the morning.

When everything was done, she took a shower, then brushed out her hair. Eventually, she was ready for bed. Though she'd brought reading material in her luggage, she decided to read the book she'd taken from the living room.

Once she'd climbed under the covers, she turned on the bedside lamp and started to read. Soon she found it hard to concentrate because she kept listening for sounds that Stefano had gone to bed, too. Inside the chalet it was quiet as a tomb. Beyond these walls the wind moaned and snow pelted the bedroom windows.

She turned off the lamp and snuggled deeper under the covers. In one way Lanza had never felt so isolated and alone, but in truth she loved it. Her life had always been planned out. Her parents had done her thinking for her. The wedding that had been organized for a year was over and now she was a married woman.

To the wrong prince.

But her parents were happy. So were his. Perhaps it meant her father's life had been preserved for a few years longer. Her thoughts wandered. Alberto would have brought her here for their honeymoon. Stefano was attempting to fulfill all his younger brother's wishes.

Before she fell asleep she wondered what her new husband would have wanted and done if he were in love with her.

When morning came Lanza walked over to the window. Snow was still falling, revealing a white world. She checked her watch: 9:40 a.m. What a surprise! She rarely slept late.

Slipping into a new pair of black wool pants and a red sweater, both of which fit her to perfection, all she had to do was fix her hair. It fell from a side part she gathered at the nape with an elastic band. After applying lipstick, she reached for Stefano's small gift and left the bedroom.

On the way down the hall she smelled coffee. She had no idea how long he'd been up because there'd been no sound. Last night she hadn't been hungry. This morning she was starving and headed for the kitchen.

Lanza found him cooking what she considered a full American breakfast. Eggs, bacon, toast. Why not? He'd received his education in Colorado. After exchanging emails for the past year, she'd learned Stefano had spent a lot of time in the States at his gold mine in South Dakota.

This morning he'd dressed in a navy hoodie and jeans that molded his powerful thighs. His five-o'clock shadow and disheveled hair added to his disturbing male presence. Her unwanted attraction to him was growing. Perhaps he'd been outside already and had worked up an appetite.

"Good morning, Stefano."

CHAPTER FIVE

STEFANO HAD BEEN wondering when his wife would awaken and make an appearance. He couldn't prevent his gaze from traveling over her beautiful face and curvaceous body, not missing one inch of her. Her long chestnut hair against the red sweater took his breath.

"Buon giorno, sposa mia."

She smiled. "You look like you slept well. What can I do to help?"

"Our food is ready. Come in the dining room and we'll eat. I've already fixed our coffee." He carried their plates and put them on the table. She followed him and placed her gift next to his food before sitting opposite him.

He eyed it with curiosity. "Am I to open this now?"

"Whenever you'd like, but I'm afraid it's not like the gift you gave me because it has no monetary value."

"Now you've intrigued me. I think I'll wait until later."

She spooned sugar into her coffee after pouring some from the carafe. Without waiting for him, she dug in and helped herself to two more helpings of bacon, which pleased him.

"This breakfast is delicious. I could get used to it. You're welcome to do all the cooking for as long as we're here."

He stopped munching on his toast. "We'll be leaving tomorrow."

"Why?"

"Because it occurred to me you might not like it up here. Alberto wasn't entirely sure, either. In that case, I've planned to drive us around some of the Mediterranean countries you mentioned you hadn't visited in your emails."

"That's very considerate of you." She finished eating everything and eventually sat back to eye him through her dark lashes. "You're an awesome bridegroom. Feed your bride an excellent meal before doing anything else. But before we discuss how to spend our honeymoon, I'd like to hear you lay out the rules of engagement."

Her response let him know she'd not forgotten that message he'd sent her a year ago. But he was in an entirely different place now.

"That wasn't my best choice of words at the time. I wish I'd put it a different way. Let's agree this situation wasn't what either of us had anticipated. For want of a better word, I see our marriage as one of convenience for a way to begin."

Her eyes pulsed a deep blue. "Didn't that quaint expression get thrown out decades ago?"

"Possibly," he murmured, wishing he hadn't used that word, either.

"Please go on and explain the details. I like the sound of it if it means we can do whatever we want and open the door of our cage to unknown possibilities."

He took a long time to finish drinking his coffee. "Not all the time. When there are public duties, we'll have to do them together."

"Naturally, but you're the one my father is going to lean on, not me," she emphasized. "He doesn't believe a woman should rule. I'm afraid you've gotten the brunt."

Stefano rubbed the back of his neck in frustration. "There'll be times when I'll have to be gone for long periods."

"You mean that you'll leave to do your engineering work and come back each time to rule when you've finished your business. In that case, when you're away I'll be able to indulge myself without anyone telling me I can't. This could work."

He frowned. "You do understand what I'm saying. For the time being we'll be living in separate bedrooms."

"Of course. I took that for granted the moment I read your missive a year ago about not having a wedding night. In fact, I assumed as much before I told my parents I would accept your proposal. How long do you see our separate bedrooms lasting?"

If she only knew he didn't want separate bedrooms. He already desired her. "Shall we say until we've become comfortable with each other?"

"That sounds reasonable. I'll admit that marrying you has already given me the freedom I didn't think I'd ever have."

"What are you insinuating?"

"Alberto and I were trapped and understood our duty." Stefano was stunned. Had she honestly felt that way when she'd been engaged to his brother? "But marriage to you under the rules you've set out means we'll both be able to do whatever we desire to a greater degree, right?"

He didn't like what she was saying. Not at all. "At some juncture we'll have to talk about having children."

She sat back. "That's true. As you said,

we need time to become comfortable with each other."

"Alberto's death changed many things for me. I find I'm looking forward to having children with you."

"Even though you gave up the royal life at eighteen?"

Stefano cocked his head. "But I took it back again to marry you. Sometimes people and circumstances change."

She eyed him over her coffee cup. "If we do this thing right, it will let us off the hook in more ways than one, *if* you know what I mean."

"I'm not sure I do," he said.

"While you're off doing gold-mining business around the world, I can be busy carrying out my charity works, which are considerable."

"Alone?"

She stared at him. "What are you implying?"

"You know what I'm asking. Has there been another important man in your life? It would be understandable, of course. I just want to be clear about where we stand."

"Only Alberto." Hearing that admission didn't help Stefano's understanding. "I'm afraid I'm one of a dying breed. Your parents and mine made sure I'm pure as the proverbial snow burying us alive as we speak.

"Alberto was my betrothed for a year. And, according to him, you were never bound to one woman. In case you only suspected it, Stefano, he adored you. The only time he truly showed passion was when he talked about you."

Her mention of Alberto had again reached a private region of his soul. Before he could say another word, she got up from the table. After taking her dishes to the counter in the kitchen, she returned to the dining room.

"I need to be excused for a few minutes, but I'll be back. Maybe now would be a good time for you to open your wedding present. When you see what's inside, you'll understand why it really should belong to

you. During the twelve months we were engaged, it's the only thing Alberto ever sent
to me."

Surprised that Alberto had anything to do
with Lanza's wedding present to him, Stefano was more bewildered than ever. Worse,
he hated that his eyes lingered on her womanly figure as she disappeared to the other
part of the chalet.

He'd never spent a more uncomfortable
hour with a woman in his life, and she was
his wife! The fact that she had an allure that
appealed to him only compounded his frustration.

Unable to concentrate on anything, he got
up from the table and cleared the rest of the
dishes. After he'd cleaned up the kitchen, he
walked back to the dining room.

Her gift lay on the table unopened. He
couldn't imagine what she might have given
him relating to his brother. The youngest
daughter of King Victor could be unpredict-
able, so it seemed.

When he realized he was making too

much of it, he undid the gold paper around the flat, three-by-four-inch box. As he lifted the lid, he saw his own face looking up at him. The black-and-white photo took him back in time. He remembered sending it to Alberto, who was always after him to send him pictures.

A friend had taken it while he was in Kenya at the mine. He drew it from the box. There was a note folded beneath it. He smoothed it out.

Dear Lanza,

After I returned home from my last visit to Domodossola, I decided to send you this photo of Stefano at twenty-two because you said you wanted to get to know me better and asked me what I treasured most.

As I told you, I've always missed him and wished he were here. No one ever had a better brother.

I'll never stop loving him and hope this helps you to understand the sad-

ness you sometimes glimpse in me. I've always considered him my other half. Life has never been quite the same without him.

Alberto

Stefano closed his eyes tightly, squeezing the paper in his hand. Gripped by emotions churning inside him, he remained there for countless minutes. When he could function, he dashed down the stairs for his ski outfit and gloves. The need to be alone propelled him outside into the storm, which hadn't abated. He was surprised it had gone on this long.

The deep snow made it difficult to walk, but he was so churned up, nothing mattered. He kept going for several hours, working off the adrenaline surging through him.

He would never have credited Lanza with enough sensitivity to give him a priceless treasure like the one in the box. Though he'd believed his parents, the note and photo to Lanza was further verification that everything they'd told him about his younger brother's desire for Stefano to be free was true.

He found himself suffering all over again for Alberto's willingness to rule while Stefano was allowed to wander the globe doing exactly what he wanted. Stefano had missed his brother, too, so much at times he'd wondered if his freedom had been worth it.

Where Lanza was concerned, he felt remorse for insinuating that she might have been unfaithful to Alberto. What in the hell had prompted him to use words that made her feel like he was treating her as an enemy with that couriered message? She'd been as much of a victim as he had.

Guilt plagued him over his behavior. He'd made her feel that she was trapped in a loveless, sexless marriage and could never have his heart because he hadn't wanted to be a royal.

During their conversation he'd meant it when he'd told her he was looking forward to having children with her. If she hadn't acted excited at the prospect, it was because she'd been guarding herself with good reason. He realized he'd done a lot of damage with his words. Those emails were a paltry excuse for the time alone they'd needed. She had every right to think of him as a beast.

While he'd been out walking in the snow, he'd been contemplating a plan to make her happy. If she wanted freedom, they would work out an arrangement.

Who was she, really?

The woman who'd exchanged vows with him yesterday had the face of an angel and eyes the color of a deep blue fjord. But after the conversation they'd exchanged at breakfast this morning—which had turned him inside out—he couldn't get her off his mind.

Had Lanza been grief-stricken at his brother's funeral, or had it been an act? Stefano would give anything to know if the wife he'd only been married to for twenty-four hours was the same woman Alberto had talked to over the year they'd been betrothed.

Enzo's words to him at the bank a year ago hadn't left his thoughts. *Let her know before you're married that you plan to be your own person and continue doing the mining work you love while you help her father govern. It'll mean you'll be apart from her for long periods. Give her time to adjust to that fact, know what I mean?*

Stefano's best friend had turned out to give him the wrong advice. That wasn't Enzo's fault. Stefano had been wrong to follow it and was the only one to blame for making Lanza feel insecure about a marriage forced on her.

To his shock it was already late afternoon by the time he made it back to the chalet. He'd been gone much longer than he'd realized and imagined he looked like the abominable snowman. But he didn't have to worry about Lanza, who hadn't been concerned how long he'd been gone, nor had she rushed downstairs even if she'd heard him come in.

When he removed his gear and eventually went upstairs, he saw her engrossed in a book on one of the couches facing the fire-place. She looked so enticing he wanted to lie down and take her in his arms.

To his chagrin there was no sign of a hysterical wife who was out of her mind with worry because she'd been left alone too long in a strange place and felt unprotected. Stefano had the deep impression she didn't know what time it was and didn't care. Again, it was all his fault. He needed to change things—and quickly.

He walked down the hall to his bedroom to freshen up. Before he joined her, he went to the closet for his overcoat. The pockets still held her high heels. He picked them up and placed them inside her bedroom door.

An odd sensation passed through him when he thought of her standing on them throughout their entire wedding day. She stood five feet four, but they'd made her taller. Taking a deep breath, he had to admit he'd found her exquisite with that lace veil covering her features in an almost seductive way.

No doubt Alberto had been attracted to her from the beginning. That would explain why it hadn't been hard to go along with the betrothal. Stefano couldn't help but wonder if Lanza had been physically drawn to his brother. Alberto, who resembled their mother, had enjoyed girlfriends behind the scenes before becoming engaged to Lanza.

Irritated because he was dwelling too much on the two of them, he headed for the living room. His wife had curled up on one end of the couch with a throw blanket covering her.

"Is that a book you brought with you?"

She turned her head to look at him with a passive gaze. "No. One of yours. It's a good spy novel."

"I'm glad you're enjoying it. In truth, I didn't mean to be gone so long."

A small smile lit her lips. "This is your world. For the last month all you've done is get ready for our wedding. But it's over at last. You can relax for a little while and do what you want from here on out. I know I'm loving the freedom."

There was that word *freedom* again. It had driven him away from his family. Now it was driving him and his new bride apart if he didn't take steps to make their marriage work.

"Are you hungry?"

She shook her head. "I ate earlier, but I imagine you are and know exactly what you're going to fix. As I told you earlier, you're a great cook."

His hands curled into fists, not because of her remarks, but because of his earlier behavior toward her. "Before any more time passes, let me thank you for the gift. The note Alberto wrote to you is priceless to me. I'll always treasure it."

"You and your brother clearly had an exceptional relationship. For you to take his place and marry me is beyond extraordinary. What you've done is almost unbelievable."

Lanza was wrong. Alberto had laid down

his life for his brother, who'd been spoiled and hadn't thought about anyone but himself. But what was almost unbelievable was Lanza's willingness to marry Stefano.

"What's extraordinary to me is that you accepted my proposal. For what it's worth, you've made me very happy, Lanza."

Her eyes finally looked away, but not before he saw them light up. Hopefully, she'd believed him.

"Tomorrow morning Enzo will be here to take us down to the city. From there we'll leave and start our trip. After ten days we'll return to Domodossola."

She sat up. "I have an even better idea. Why don't you plan to go where you want while I visit Zia Ottavia in Rome? She invited me to come at the wedding. I promise I won't tell a soul." So saying, she went back to her novel.

He'd never been dismissed before. That was what it felt like. But in truth, he'd been the one to set the rules. Damn if she hadn't taken him at his word on everything, but this was going to change. He planned to change the rules until she welcomed him in her arms and her bed.

After making some sandwiches and coffee, he disappeared down the hall to his bedroom for the night. A ton of work had piled up while he'd been getting ready for his marriage. He dug in and arranged for his next travel plans to include the Casale mine in South America.

But to his chagrin, he had a devil of a time staying focused on his work. He kept replaying her unexpected remarks in his head. It wasn't as much what she said as the tone of her delivery. In his gut he knew that somewhere deep inside her lovely facade lived the real Lanza. He was convinced that neither he nor Alberto had ever met her.

Lanza woke up the next morning to discover sunshine had filled the bedroom. Loving the light, she scrambled out of bed and padded over to the window. A blue sky had chased away the blizzard.

Glorious, dazzling snow resembling trillions of diamonds covered Stefano's playground. That was what it was, and secretly she loved this hideaway of his. Wouldn't every man or woman kill to live in such splendid isolation? This was her childhood dream come true. She had always fantasized about having freedom from her royal life. And here there was no one dogging her footsteps or telling her what she could and couldn't do.

More than anything she wanted to go out and play in the scrumptious white stuff no human had touched. She'd give anything to stay longer. If only Enzo weren't coming. Nothing sounded worse than having to leave on a driving trip to fill time when they had paradise right here.

If she only could stay, Lanza would borrow some of Stefano's winter clothes and fix them so they'd fit. Luckily, he'd bought her boots. In her dreams she'd go outside for hours and have a blast. Too bad that wasn't going to happen.

Knowing that Enzo could be here at any moment, she showered and put on another sweater and pair of wool pants. Once she'd done her hair and makeup, she made her bed and packed her bags. It had surprised her that she'd found her high heels inside the door when she'd gone to bed last night. She smiled when she remembered Stefano putting them in his elegant coat pockets.

With everything done, she reached for her coat and carried her cases down the hall to the living room. There was no sign of Stefano, but she noticed that his cases had been placed near the stairs. She put her things there, too. Maybe he was outside waiting for Enzo.

Lanza walked into the kitchen that looked spotless. She reached for a small apple in the bowl on the counter. While she ate it, she wandered over to the living room windows. Once again her breath caught at the beauty of the Alps in winter. Then a noise from below caused her to turn around. She saw her husband walk into the room with a concerned expression.

"*Buon giorno*, Stefano."

His gaze traveled over her in that way that told her he missed nothing. It made her feel fluttery inside.

"*Buon giorno*, Lanza."

"I'm all packed and ready to go. Has Enzo arrived?"

He shook his dark head. "He's late and there's no cell phone service. The storm must have knocked it out along with the electricity. There's no email, either."

So *that was* what was wrong. But the news couldn't have made her happier. "How long have you been outside waiting?"

"About an hour. I walked to the gate in case he couldn't get in and shoveled, but I didn't see him. There were no cars going in either direction."

"I'm sure he'll be here as soon as he can. Have you eaten yet?"

"No. I'd planned to take you to brunch after we got back to the city."

He had no idea how delighted she was to have to stay here longer. "Since we don't know how long we'll have to wait for him, I'll fix us some frittata." Lanza loved an omelet eaten with the kind of crusty Italian bread he had on hand. "You have a generator, right?"

He blinked. "You noticed—"

"I can even cook when I have to."

The first real smile she'd seen broke out on his handsome face. So…food played an important part in his life, *if* he didn't have to make it. Or maybe he did like to cook, having been on his own all these years.

"I'll go downstairs and turn it on." Soon she heard the sound of the generator. They had power.

She removed her coat and walked through to the kitchen to put her apple core in the wastebasket. Next, she made coffee. After finding a bowl and pan, she reached for eggs and other ingredients out of the fridge to start their meal. Before long she'd made large, fluffy ham and cheese omelets cooked in butter.

Because he'd stocked the fridge with items for salad, she added mushrooms, red peppers and chives. Once everything was ready, she prepared two plates that overflowed with chunks of the bread and put them on the table.

Stefano appeared in time to carry the coffee and silverware to the dining room. He eyed the food. "These look fabulous."

"The palace kitchen staff taught me and my sisters how to cook from the time we were little."

They both started to eat. His food disappeared in a hurry. "They taught you well. This is the best omelet I've ever tasted."

"Thank you. You want me to make you another one?"

"Would you?"

They were good if she said so herself. "I want another one, too. I'm starving."

Quickly, she went to the kitchen and whipped up another batch. He brought their plates to the stove, and she slid the cooked food onto them. "Uh-oh," she cried. He chuckled because one of the omelets almost slid away from her.

Lanza happened to look up at him and caught the intense way he was staring at her out of those beautiful black eyes. She quivered in reaction, wishing he would kiss her. She wanted to feel his mouth on hers. What was happening to her?

Back at the table they dug in once more. But she could only eat half of hers and shoved her plate toward him so he'd finish it, which he did, as well as the rest of the bread.

When she saw him pull out his cell phone to make a call, Lanza got up to clear the table and do the dishes. He followed her into the kitchen. "There's still no service."

"Do you often have blackouts here in winter?"

"No. This is very unusual." He put the leftover ingredients back in the fridge while she loaded the dishwasher. "I'll check to see if Enzo has emailed me."

"That's a good idea."

He returned to the kitchen a minute later. "No message yet. Something tells me Enzo won't be coming today."

CHAPTER SIX

YES! LANZA DIDN'T want to leave.

She was loving this time with Stefano and didn't want anything to change. "It's so beautiful out. Do you have some winter clothes for outside I could borrow?"

Her question seemed to take him by surprise. "There's a closet downstairs with my sister, Carla's, ski outfit and skis. She's a little taller than you, but I'm sure they'll fit. You're welcome to use them."

"Thank you."

"Come with me and I'll show you."

She trailed him to the lower level where he opened a closet with half a dozen outfits. He pulled out a woman's stylish white parka and black ski pants. He found her everything—gloves, a white ski hat, ski socks and boots.

Elated, she stepped into the pants and put on the socks and boots. Then she zipped up the parka and tugged the wool hat over her head. Everything fit just fine.

"You look perfect, Lanza." In the next instant he kissed her briefly on the mouth the way she'd wanted when they were in the kitchen. Her heart almost palpitated out of her parka.

While she pulled on her gloves, she looked over and noticed him getting on his ski clothes. "Where are you going?"

His eyes roved over her, setting her on fire. "Outside with you." Her heart turned over. It hadn't occurred to her that he might come with her, though she wanted him to be with her with every atom of her body. "Have you ever been snowshoeing?"

"Never."

"This is the perfect kind of snow for it." He reached for the snowshoes. "Come outside with me and I'll help you put them on."

Lanza walked out into the brilliant sunlight, thrilled to be entering this glistening white world with Stefano, who'd just kissed her because he'd wanted to. Maybe some dreams could come true.

With her pulse racing, she leaned against his broad shoulder while he knelt down to center her boot in the binding. She never expected to be doing something this exciting with her handsome husband, who was taking amazing care of her.

He wrapped the heel strap around the back and through the buckle to tighten it. "Does that feel snug?"

"Yes."

"Now we'll do your other foot." Within a minute she was ready. "Keep your legs apart as you start to take steps. It requires more energy than you'll be used to, but it won't take long for you to work into a rhythm."

While she experimented, he went inside for his snowshoes and came back, shutting the door. In seconds he'd fastened his straps with a finesse that revealed years of experience. She gave him a covert glance because she couldn't stop herself from looking at him.

Her husband really was a gorgeous male no matter what he wore. Lanza found herself wildly attracted to him. She'd never expected this to happen and it shocked her that she wanted him so badly in every way.

Lanza took off across the front property of the chalet toward the white shrouded pines in the distance. Stefano caught up to her within seconds.

"Where's the fire?"

The last thing she wanted him to know was that his kiss had set off an explosion inside her. She wanted more. So much more. "I'm just excited to be out here making fresh tracks. It's a surreal feeling, as if we're on top of the world."

"I love it, too."

She could tell he did. In time, they came to the trees. Lanza kept going, marveling over the sculptures created by the wind and snow.

As they penetrated deeper, she thought she

heard a yapping sound. She stopped walking and turned to Stefano. "Did you hear that?"

"I did." He reached out to grasp her arm with his gloved hand in a protective movement. "Don't go any farther."

"If I didn't know better, I would think it was a dog."

He shook his head. "Not a dog."

"Whatever it is, it sounds wounded."

"Wait here while I go look." Again, she was touched that he wanted to keep her safe. But the second he let go of her and went on ahead, she hurried to catch up. The yapping continued. Two hundred feet farther along, she saw him approach a small animal with red fur and a snout half buried in the snow beneath the boughs of a fat pine tree.

"Oh, Stefano, it's a little fox." She couldn't imagine it weighing more than seven or eight pounds.

"Stay back, Lanza."

"They're not dangerous and it can't hurt anybody. Listen. It's in pain." She pulled off her gloves so she could remove her parka.

"Wrap it inside my coat to keep it warm and we'll take it back to the chalet."

"Lanza—" he muttered in exasperation.

"Don't worry about me. I'll be fine in this sweater. Please—we've got to help it before it's too late. It's so sweet."

To her relief he swaddled it like a baby and stood up. The fox kept yapping. She put her gloves back on and together they returned to the chalet as fast as they could go. "It must have gotten injured during the storm and couldn't go any farther."

When they reached the entrance, it was her turn to help Stefano. "I'll undo your snowshoes so you can take it inside to the fireplace." She got down and unfastened his straps so he was free to go in. It was a pleasure doing something for him when he was doing everything for her including taking care of the fox.

Another minute and she stepped out of her snowshoes. Then she carried all four of them inside and shut the door before going upstairs. Stefano had found a blanket where he laid the yapping fox and kept the parka over it to retain warmth. She turned on the switch that lit the fire, then knelt down beside him.

"The poor thing is frightened and needs food. I'll warm some milk. I could dip a cloth in it and then let it drip into his mouth. What do you think?"

"I think you're the most amazing woman I've ever known."

His compliment filled her with warmth. "Why do you say that?"

"Your kindness and lack of fear. Your concern for a wild animal. All of it."

"I could say exactly the same thing about you." Quickly, she hurried to the kitchen and warmed a pan of milk. After finding a clean washcloth, she carried the items over to the blanket.

"If you'll force its mouth open, I'll squeeze the liquid into it."

For the next hour they worked together feeding the fox, who eventually stopped yapping.

Stefano's eyes smiled into hers at last.

"He's still alive thanks to your quick thinking, Lanza. I believe you got a cup of milk down him."

"Him?"

A chuckle escaped his lips.

"It may not be enough. Don't tell your sister what we did with her parka, Stefano."

"When I brag about what you did, she'll never mind. If you'll stay right here, I'll find a box and make a bed for him. He'll feel safer and more comfortable if he's enclosed."

"Do you think he's been injured?"

"That's hard to tell, but I don't think so."

"Maybe he developed hypothermia."

"That's possible." After he disappeared down the stairs, she checked beneath the parka. The fox was warming up and stirred at the touch of her hand. In a minute, Stefano returned with a two-by-three-foot carton. He gathered the blanket holding the fox and placed it inside.

She tucked the parka around it before

glancing at Stefano. "His home has to be somewhere near the chalet. If we can get him strong enough, he can be released."

Stefano studied her features. "I didn't know you went to vet school," he drawled.

Lanza smiled. "Nothing so admirable. When we were young my sisters and I often found injured creatures and birds around the estate and nursed them, but it had to remain a secret. Fausta was a natural tending them, but *Mamà* didn't want us touching wild things that had diseases. Our parents were too protective of us."

"Don't they know you're fearless?"

"You should see Donetta in action. She's a real warrior. The way she rides a horse, you would think she was born on one and has won every international *concorso* she's ever been in. Her trophies need their own room to be displayed. My sister would make a great king."

"King?"

"Yes. The word *queen* loses too much in the translation for her."

Deep, rich laughter burst out of Stefano, the kind she loved.

"From my earliest memories of her, she has always wanted to rule. But not with a husband! That's probably the real reason she didn't get picked to be Alberto's intended in the first place. As for Fausta, she has always refused the idea of marrying a prince. She intends to find a man of the people in the city. That left *moi*."

Stefano started to say something, then seemed to think the better of it.

"If my father would have that absurd ancient rule changed proclaiming only a man can rule, Donetta would make the perfect head of Domodossola. She's brilliant and innovative. That would be really lucky for you since you'd be free to spend even more time away doing your thing."

Lanza had only told him she would like to go to her aunt's while he did what he wanted, because she was afraid to spend any more time with him. Now she was growing increasingly drawn to her husband, which was dangerous. She'd be a fool to enjoy any more of his company when she feared he could never fall madly in love with her. That was what she wanted.

CHAPTER SEVEN

MY THING?

Here Stefano had been feeling comfortable with Lanza for the first time since their wedding and she suddenly interjected a discordant note. Did she mean his mining business or something else? If it was the latter, then she had every right to question his future associations with women. He'd insinuated the same thing about her relationships with other men during her betrothal to Alberto.

"It's a good thing you stocked milk. Are you a big milk drinker, Stefano?"

"Yes. I like it with my muesli. Sometimes it's all I eat when I'm busy. Since I didn't know if you wanted some, I made sure we had it on hand."

"That was lucky for Fausto."

He angled his head at her. "Fausto?"

"Yes. I've named him that because it means lucky. Our little fox was lucky Enzo didn't come for us and we were able to find him." Lanza stood up. "I'm going to heat more milk." She left his side and walked into the kitchen with the empty pan and rag.

Stefano stared into the flames. Something unprecedented was happening to him since his wedding day. He realized he was becoming enamored of his wife and wanted her in all the ways a man wanted a woman.

When he'd committed to marrying her, he'd promised himself to make it work, but his desire for her had already happened. She had a charm that took him by complete surprise.

Thank heaven something had prevented Enzo from making it up here. It gave him and Lanza more time together in his favorite place on earth. He could tell she loved it here, too, and he wanted their honeymoon to begin in earnest. Since it would be another day before Enzo arrived, Stefano was excited at the thought of spending more time alone with Lanza.

She returned and they again started the process of squeezing milk into the mouth he eased open. "Look—Fausto's tongue is curling around the drops. He *likes* it!" she cried in real pleasure. The fox was coming back to life. "At this rate I think he'll want some solid food before long."

Her caring and tenderness reached a place in his soul he didn't know was there.

She lifted jewel-blue eyes to him. "It's almost time for dinner. I'll fix some ham sandwiches and feed him part of mine. Do you think he should have ham?"

He grinned. "If not, we'll find out."

Again, she carried the pan and cloth to the kitchen. While she was gone, the fox stirred enough that Stefano removed the parka so it could have more breathing room. It lay on its side, but he could see it trying to right itself. More food would make a difference.

Before long she returned to kneel by him. "Your sandwiches are on the counter."

"Thank you, but first I want to help you by opening its mouth so you can put some ham on its tongue."

She teased the fox by dangling a small piece of meat in front of its nose. That brought out its tongue. Lanza pushed the ham inside and they kept up the process until all the ham in her sandwich was gone.

Stefano chuckled. "It's working. He likes it."

"Now *I'm* the one starving to death."

"I'll get up and make you another sandwich. Then we'll eat here together to keep him company."

Before long he was back with their food and a small, shallow bowl of water. Stefano put it in a corner of the box near its head. He sprinkled some on its snout and it produced a reaction. The fox moved its head and pretty soon they watched it start to lick the water.

"Oh—you're thirsty, aren't you?" She looked at Stefano. "Do you think he would like some of your muesli?"

"Probably. I'll put a little in another bowl and we'll see what happens."

Within an hour the fox had turned over on its own and was eating and drinking.

"By morning we might be able to put him outside the chalet with more food and water and see what he does. If he seems fit, I'll carry him back to that tree where we found him so he can find his way home."

"I'll help you because I know it's the right thing to do, but I'd love to keep him for a pet." Her eyes focused on the fox. "He's so sweet. I hope Enzo doesn't come for a long time. That way I can keep an eye on Fausto and know he's going to be all right until we have to go."

It was getting late. Instinct told him Enzo wouldn't be coming tonight. "If you want to go to bed, I'll stay up with the fox for a while."

She turned her head toward him. "I was going to say the same thing. I know you always have mining business to take care of and we've got internet now because of the generator. I'll stay right here by the fire a few more minutes so he knows he's not alone."

Stefano had a feeling she knew how attracted he was to her and wanted to kiss her, but he decided not to press it yet. "Then I'll say good-night and see you in the morning." He leaned over to kiss her cheek. "*Buona notte*, Lanza."

He got up from the floor and headed for his bedroom. The first thing he did was shower and get ready for bed in his navy sweats. Anything to take his mind off his delectable wife sitting in the firelight.

Next, he went over to his desk and discovered that Enzo had just sent him an email.

Stefano, a major blizzard has hit the area and thousands are without power. Including me until I could start up our generator. Worse, there was an avalanche that has covered the road two miles south of you. It could be close to a week before it's passable again because there are too many other areas in much more need of help. I'll come as soon as I can. If you need help before then, I can notify your father to send a helicopter for you. Please advise.

He took a deep breath before responding. In his gut he knew Lanza didn't want to be rescued and not just because of the fox.

Enzo. Thank you, but there's no reason for urgency. Don't tell anyone where we are. Let me know your schedule when you know more. S.

While he waited to hear back, he left his bedroom to tell Lanza the news.

The sight before his eyes caused him to stop in his tracks. Her lovely body lay on its side by the box sound asleep. She had an angelic look in profile. The lambent flames from the fire brought out the strands of reddish gold in her luxurious chestnut hair. Stefano had the desire to run his hands through it.

Much as he'd like to lie down next to her,

he didn't dare for too many reasons to consider. He could try to wake her up, but she probably wouldn't appreciate being disturbed. The news from Enzo could wait till morning. On impulse, he left to get a blanket for her and turn down the fire.

The fox had been curled up, but immediately lifted its head when Stefano drew near to cover her. Who was guarding whom? A smile broke the corner of his mouth before he stole back to his room for the rest of the night.

In case she needed him, he left his door open and went to bed. But he didn't sleep well because he kept listening for any sounds from her or the fox. When morning came he got dressed and shaved, eager to find out what was going on in the living room.

He found Lanza on her knees once more, hand-feeding some bits of apple to their patient with all the joy of a child at the zoo. She saw Stefano out of the corner of her eye.

"I thought you'd sleep longer."

"I couldn't until I knew how you got on. We have news, Lanza. Enzo sent me an email late last night. The storm knocked out the electricity and triggered an avalanche farther down the mountain. There are so many other regions needing emergency assistance, he's heard it might be a week before the road is cleared. He'll come to get us as soon as he can, but we might have a long wait."

Her smile widened, telling him everything he wanted to know. "Thank you for the blanket you threw over me. Because of it I had a wonderful sleep."

"That's good. I'll get Fausto some more food and water." He reached for the empty bowls and went to the kitchen. After replenishing the dishes, he brought them back to the box.

"Look how hungry he is!" she cried.

He nodded. "The ham didn't bother him. Now it's time I fixed our own breakfast."

Stefano went back to the kitchen to make scrambled eggs and bacon. She came in to fix the coffee and toast. In a few minutes they sat down to eat at the dining room table.

"I'll admit I'm glad we've been given more time to stay here."

"Me, too," he murmured. She had no idea. "We have a lot to talk about. I've wanted to explain the reason I didn't come to visit you this past year."

She lifted searching eyes to him. "Why didn't you?"

"I knew you were trying to get over Alberto's death. So was I. Though we agreed to get married and please our parents, I felt like you and I needed the past year apart to sort out our feelings before meeting again. I was half-afraid that seeing me before the wedding would have made you run the other way."

"By now you know that's not true," she laughed gently.

"But I was wrong to stay away."

"No," she countered. "Not wrong. It's true

I was in limbo, but the emails really helped me get a sense of your life."

"The same for me, Lanza."

"I'm glad things worked out this way."

He covered her hand and squeezed it. "You really mean that?"

"Yes."

"Then let's go downstairs and get ready to enjoy this day."

She followed him below. He opened the closet door for her. A few minutes later she appeared in his sister's ski outfit. Her womanly figure drew his attention. No matter what she wore, he found himself unable to keep his eyes off his new wife.

He carried the box outside with some food. "If you want, we'll put on our snowshoes and trek across the property to that pine tree. Maybe he'll follow us. I'll tuck a bag of food inside my parka in case he trails us."

Together they strapped themselves into their snowshoes and started across the expanse, retracing their own former tracks that stood out in the snow. Every so often they looked back, but the fox had stayed in the box. Eventually, they reached the pine tree where they'd found Fausto.

Lanza shot him a guilty glance. "Maybe I did the wrong thing to feed him. Now he's spoiled and doesn't want to leave our protection."

He put his hands on his hips. "You did the right thing. Not everyone would have done that."

She bit her lip. "But it might have been a mistake." In the next breath she turned and started walking farther into the trees. She handled the snowshoes like a pro.

"Stefano!"

Her cry drew his attention and he started after her. It was an older stand of forest. He noticed a lot of debris and some trees had been downed during the ferocity of the storm. "What is it?"

"I need your help."

Alarmed, he hurried toward the sound of her voice. When he came upon her, she was standing at the end of a toppled tree that was dead in spots. "What's wrong?"

"This top would make the perfect Christmas tree. If we could break it off, we could drag it back to the chalet and pretend it's Christmas Eve. All the pine cones make perfect ornaments. Thanks to the wedding, I feel like Christmas passed me by this year."

He stared at her in disbelief. "You didn't celebrate Christmas?"

"We had a tree at the palace, but getting ready for the wedding took precedence over everything. I feel like I missed it altogether. From childhood I dreamed of finding my own little tree in the woods near the palace and putting it in my room. But that was never allowed." She averted her eyes. "Please forget I said anything. It was a silly idea."

With a flushed face, she worked her way past him to reach the clearing.

Stefano walked over to the tree and took a good look to see if separating it was possible. After bracing his boot against the dead part near the top, he grasped the trunk and pulled hard. To his surprise it gave. He kept tugging until he pulled it free.

The little tree couldn't be more than five feet in length, light and easy enough to pull behind him. Over the years he'd often spent the holidays at the chalet, but he'd never put up a tree, let alone one from his own property. The novel idea seemed to be important to his wife and he wanted to please her. When he got it back to the chalet, he could fix a stand for it and set it up in the living room.

All these years he'd put off the idea of getting married because he loved being free. When he thought about it, he realized that the relationships he'd sought over the years had always fallen short of anything lasting.

Though his mother had hit a nerve, she hadn't been off the mark when she'd reminded him he hadn't brought a special woman home for them to meet. That was her argument to convince him he had no reason not to marry Lanza and fulfill his duty.

But now he was beginning to think that wasn't the real reason that had stopped him from settling down. Maybe it was possible that the only reason he'd remained single this long was because he'd never met the right woman until Lanza...

CHAPTER EIGHT

LANZA KEPT WALKING toward the chalet, feeling like a fool. It had been the height of idiocy to talk to him about a Christmas tree. He must think she was stupid. But she knew she'd fallen in love with her husband and was living out her private fantasy of sharing Christmas with the man she wanted to spend the rest of her life with.

As she trudged on, there was no sign of Fausto. Maybe he'd run away while they'd been gone. That would be a good thing. He belonged in the wild.

Maybe her eyes were deceiving her, but when she reached the chalet she saw the fox creep out of the box, almost as if he was greeting her.

"Fausto—I thought you were gone." He moved around, keeping his distance, but he didn't run off. "You're not ready to go home yet and I suspect you're hungry. Don't worry. We'll feed you in a minute."

She removed her snowshoes and took them inside. When she went back out, she was met with another surprise. In the distance she saw Stefano's tall, striking physique coming closer. He dragged the little tree behind him that he'd broken off for her.

The trouble he'd gone to in order to make her happy caught at her heart. This husband of hers was turning out to be a very different person from the man she'd envisioned.

"You didn't have to do this."

He lowered it to the snow and shot her a penetrating glance. "I've never put up a Christmas tree in the chalet before. It'll be a first for me. I like the idea that we're doing this together to set a tradition. How's our fox?"

"He's been waiting for us. I'm sure he's hungry."

"Go ahead and feed him while I erect a stand for the tree." Stefano reached inside his parka and handed her the bag of food.

While he took off his snowshoes, she put some of the food in the dish. The fox must have smelled it because he hurried over to the box and began to eat. "Yup. I've ruined him. While you're busy, I'll go inside and get dinner started."

She went inside to remove her ski clothes, then hurried upstairs to turn on the fireplace before going to the kitchen. They'd been out much longer than she'd realized. Stefano had to be starving, too. She'd seen some filet mignon steaks she could thaw and decided to make cheese dumplings. Along with potatoes and onions to cook, she would put a salad together.

While she'd been preparing their meal, Stefano had come upstairs several times. Once to bring up the box with Fausto, then the tree that he stood in one corner of the living room against the window.

He'd brought Christmas inside, thrilling her.

The sight of him placing it in the right position appealed to her deepest emotions and fulfilled fantasies she'd never thought would come true.

After he disappeared again, she found a bottle of red wine on the shelf and put it on the table. Soon she had it set and brought out two wineglasses. Lanza also lighted two candles ensconced in brass holders from one of the end tables and used them for a centerpiece. Everything was set.

Since he still hadn't appeared, she hurried to her bedroom to change into a blue silk blouse and khaki pants. After brushing her hair so that it fell from a side part, she left it undone and put on her pink frost lipstick. Now she felt more presentable.

When she left the bedroom, she almost ran into Stefano, who was just coming out of his room. He'd shaved and looked so incredibly attractive in a black silk shirt and trousers, her legs came close to buckling.

His dark gaze enveloped her, sending heat throughout her body. "I wondered where the cook had gone. Something smells wonderful."

They headed for the living room. "I made cheese dumplings. They'll be done in five minutes." She'd wanted to make something special for him. Heaven help her, but her desire for him was becoming overwhelming. She couldn't believe she was the same woman who before coming to the chalet had considered her life a disaster area.

Stefano put more water in a bowl for Fausto while she fixed their dinner plates and took them to the table. "Come and eat while everything is hot."

It amused her to watch him devour all his dumplings first. After he put down his fork, his eyes bored into hers. "I've never tasted dumplings like these before and could eat the whole pan."

"I like them, too. Bianca, the head cook, says they're her signature recipe."

"I can see why."

"Sometimes she makes them with spinach."

"I prefer them just the way they are. In

fact, this whole dinner is exceptional. You're an excellent cook."

"Thank you."

He opened the wine and poured some into their glasses. Then he lifted his in her direction. *"Felice Anno Nuovo, Signora Casale."*

He'd just called her Mrs. Casale, reminding her she was his wife. It seemed he hadn't minded her using the name, after all. The words sent a delicious shiver down her spine. She picked up her glass in salute.

"Our New Year has swept in with an apocalyptic force. Who would have thought we'd be spending it with a little red creature and a broken off treetop? Thank you for going to that trouble. The tree makes the room more festive."

There was a glimmer in his eyes that melted her bones. "So do the candles and the wine." She could tell he wanted to get on a more intimate footing, and she knew she'd like that, too. But she couldn't prevent feeling anxious about the future. It was lovely being together while they were snowed in.

Once they returned to Domodossola and he was free to make plans, they might not have this closeness again.

"Stefano, can we talk frankly this evening?" She needed some answers.

He cast her a level glance. "Isn't that what we've been doing?"

"Before you heard that Alberto had been killed, what was your situation at the time? I'm not talking about your business affairs. I imagine you might have been involved with a woman you possibly loved. If that was the case, the shock of having to leave her and fly home to your family to deal with your pain had to have devastated you."

Lines carved his features. "Tell me something first. I know gossip abounds, but what makes you think there's been a particular one?"

"It's a natural assumption." Before he could say anything else, she asked him another question. "Before the wedding, did you have time to see her one more time? If there was a woman, there would have been so much to discuss about the huge change in your life that meant taking on your royal duty by marrying me."

"I don't like that word," he bit out.

Heat filled her cheeks. "Neither do I, but that's what it was," she fired back. "We both knew what was ahead of us, and now it's done. But the real test of living has only begun. I'm asking about your love life because I'm concerned. Four days after the funeral my father told me you'd asked for my hand in marriage.

"If there was a woman you were close to, then you weren't able to see her in person before our fathers set the seal on our marriage. Were you able to fly over and spend time with her during the year?

"If so, I can't imagine how she would have handled it. Is it possible she'll try to hurt you in some way and cause damage to our marriage that will be all over the media? If you and I hope to endure a lifetime together, then I would like to be aware of what we could be up against."

"You're afraid of public scandal?"

"I don't want to be."

He poured both of them more wine and swallowed part of his. "I'm prepared to give you all the honesty in me. I've known my share of beautiful, exciting women, but never lived with one. To answer your question, *if* I'd found the woman you're talking about—the one I couldn't live without—I'd be married by now. Believe me, there's no one out there who's going to make trouble."

"Thank you for that reassurance." She swallowed the rest of her wine. "My case is different because there was no other man from the moment I was betrothed."

"Not even a special man before?"

"No."

"Then can we talk about my brother for a minute? How did you feel about losing Alberto?"

Lanza had wondered how much he'd thought about it. His probing question, demanding an honest answer, had taken them to the heart of the matter.

"The shock of his death was one thing. But not having been in love, I didn't grieve over him. Of course I liked and admired him. The only way I can explain is that I felt guilt because I hadn't experienced acute grief. My parents were very upset I didn't fall to pieces over the news."

Stefano shook his head. "No one on the outside would expect you to feel grief since you and my brother didn't have a relationship like a man and wife."

"I'm glad you understand that, but we're talking about you. Your case is totally different because you've enjoyed a nonroyal life and have probably been intimate with a woman, which would only be natural.

"Now that I know the truth about you, will you humor me with a little more honesty and tell me how you felt about Alberto having to marry me?"

He took another drink of wine. "I didn't consider it until I fell for a local girl before going into the military. That was the first time I'd given his betrothal any serious thought and it gutted me to the point that I never stopped feeling sorry for him."

His frankness made her smile. "Did you tell him as much?"

"Yes. Every chance I got. But when I could see that my needling didn't make a dent in his good nature, I eventually stopped and tried not to think about it anymore."

"Alberto wasn't the flappable type."

"He was my total opposite. Now it's my turn. How did your sisters feel about your having to be the sacrificial lamb?"

She chuckled to hide her pain. "Donetta was overjoyed not to be in my shoes. Fausta pitied me because I was the baby. She teased me for always minding our parents."

"Why did you?"

Her delicate brows lifted. "Mind them, you mean?"

He nodded.

Stefano didn't know her father was ill. If she told him that was why she'd agreed to this marriage, it could change things. He'd hoped to have a lot of freedom to travel for his work. She wanted that same freedom, too, which was why she had no intention of telling him the truth.

"Donetta said it was because I didn't have a backbone."

His eyes narrowed on her mouth. "Donetta doesn't have a clue who you are."

Neither did Lanza, but being married to Stefano had thrust her into a whole new realm of existence. She was praying for this marriage to work. At the moment she appreciated him for being forthright. She could live with that when he was around, which wouldn't be that often.

While she was deep in thought she heard a little yip. For a while she'd forgotten about the fox. "Sounds like he wants attention." She got up from the table to give Fausto a few bits of her steak. "Uh-oh. You're out of food again."

Stefano pushed himself away from the table and stood up. "I'll fix him some more muesli and apple bits. Tomorrow I'm taking him to the tree and leaving him. He's too dependent on us already."

"I hope he has family close. What will he do if he finds himself alone?"

"Survive like all of his species."

"I want to believe you."

The tremor in Lanza's voice found its way to Stefano's heart. So did the concerns she'd voiced for fear of scandal from his past that could hurt them. More than ever he needed to do everything he could to reassure her he meant them to enjoy a loving, wonderful marriage.

After he'd prepared more food for Fausto, he did the dishes with her. When it came to the dumplings pan, he finished what was left before putting it in the dishwasher and saved one for later. "They're better than dessert," he quipped when he caught her smiling at him. Soon their work was done. She blew out the candles.

Now that darkness had crept over the mountains, Lanza went back into the living room. She spread a blanket on the floor by the box and sat next to it so she could see inside.

He walked over to the breakfront and reached for a deck of cards. "How about a game?" he asked and found a spot next to her.

She took a look at them. "Judging by how well-worn they are, I don't know that I dare play with you."

"Just a few hands of Scopa."

Lanza flashed him a mischievous smile. "Do your best."

He dealt three cards and the game began. The idea was to sweep the board and take tricks until you accrued eleven points. Right away she started to outplay him and he knew he was confronting an expert. For the next hour they were fully engaged and he'd never had so much fun in his life.

"You play like an old salt. Who taught you?"

"The head gardener's father, Duccio. He was in the merchant marines and was an invalid with a bad leg. After his wife died, I used to go to their cottage on the estate with a treat for him and he'd teach me to play all sorts of card games.

"Being with Duccio made me realize the plight of the disabled navy men who ought to have more health care and financial help after serving their country."

Stefano flicked her a glance. "I don't know who was more brilliant, the teacher or the pupil. You'll have to introduce me."

"I can't." A somber expression broke out on her face. "Duccio died last year."

"I'm sorry."

"So am I. He was a good friend who could tell the most amazing tales and kept me mesmerized."

No doubt she'd brought sunshine into his life. "Is his son a cardsharp, too?"

"No. Antonio says they're a waste of time when there's a world of growing things to cultivate and provide beauty."

Her imitation of his words and the way he

said them made Stefano laugh. The sound brought Fausto's head up.

"Oh, he's so adorable," she crooned.

Fausto wasn't the only adorable creature in the living room. "You've made a friend, Lanza."

"I know. It's got me worried."

"Tomorrow we'll try to wean him so he'll survive on his own. For now I'm going to take him downstairs. He'll be warm enough down there." Stefano wanted Lanza's complete attention and the fox needed to be on his own. "I'll be right back."

In a few minutes he'd returned. "I want a rematch of Scopa to repair the dent to my ego."

This time she made a sound of protest. "You don't fool me. I bet you let me win."

"I swear I didn't! Don't you trust me?"

Her eyes fused with his. "Of course I do."

His heart thundered in his chest. "I'm glad. Your turn first."

They played a long match. "You won, Stefano."

"It was a hard-fought battle. Now I want to claim my prize." She'd been lying on her stomach to play. Before giving her any time to think, he lay down next to her and rolled her into him. "I've been waiting to do this all night."

So saying, he lowered his mouth to kiss her the way he'd been dreaming about since that chaste kiss at the altar. She had a mouth to die for and he couldn't get enough of her. He was feverish with longing, loving the feel of her body and her response that was giving him a heart attack.

"Lanza—" He was breathless with desire. "You have no idea how delightful you are." In the next breath he tangled his legs with hers and pulled her on top of him. It was heaven to plunge his fingers into her fabulous long hair and kiss the daylights out of her.

"Stefano…" she murmured.

"I'm going too fast, aren't I, *bellissima*?" The hardest thing he'd ever had to do was stop making love to her. But she wasn't quite ready, so he moved her off him gently, allowing her to get to her feet before he did. His wife swayed a little and looked thoroughly kissed.

With her eyes glazed over she said, "*Dormi bene*, Stefano."

In a flash, she disappeared from the room, leaving him bereft. Being alone with Lanza had set off a fire that brought him alive in a whole new way. He hadn't been ready to call it a night. Far from it. They'd actually been communicating on a level he hadn't expected to happen this soon.

He gathered the scattered cards and put them away, but his body was trembling. Once he'd folded the blanket and put it on a chair, he turned down the fire.

Letting out a tormented sound, he headed for his bedroom, knowing he wouldn't be able to sleep for a long time. Thank goodness he could get on his computer, but she had nothing. It made him feel guilty.

He paused outside her door. Of course

there was no sound. On a whim, he knocked on it.

"Lanza? Would you like my radio to listen to? I have plenty of batteries."

After ten seconds he heard, "You're sure you don't want it?"

She needed help going to sleep, too. "I'm positive. Give me a minute and I'll put it by your door."

"Thank you. *Sogni d'oro*, Stefano."

"Sweet dreams to you, too, *sposa mia*."

He hurried into his room and brought the transistor radio to her door. He knocked once more. "It's here. Enjoy." After putting it down, he went back to his room and shut the door.

After getting ready for bed in a fresh pair of sweats, he sat down to a new batch of emails. Enzo had sent another update a few minutes ago, but nothing had changed in terms of the mountain road being cleared. Among the messages was one that came from the Casale Mining Company near Zacatecas, Mexico.

He hadn't been there for four months and wouldn't be going again for another four or five. The message was sent from Alicia Montoya, the only woman he'd been intimate with for a short time in the past three years. She worked in the main office, but he hadn't given her a thought in all this time.

Stefano let out a small groan. From the moment he'd learned she had a husband and hadn't told him, he'd stopped seeing her because he had no desire to get involved with a married woman.

He found out she and her husband lived apart, but they couldn't divorce because of religious reasons. Stefano understood her pain, but the revelation had changed the situation for him. Unfortunately, she had access to the files in the office.

Stefano, I have to see you. We must talk. I've been confiding in my priest. He thinks a divorce might be possible because I've lived apart from Julio for over a year with no hope of reconciliation. Answer me back and tell me you still want to be with me. I can't bear this separation from you any longer. Alicia.

He rubbed the back of his neck while he gathered his thoughts. There'd been a time when he'd enjoyed Alicia's company. But even if he hadn't gotten married and Alicia was now divorced, Stefano knew it had never been an affair of the heart and wouldn't endure.

The fact that she hadn't told him she was still married caused his feelings to undergo a complete change. It wasn't difficult for him to compose his answer.

Alicia, if it's a divorce you want, I hope it's granted for your sake, so you can be happy. But my circumstances have changed. I'm now a happily married man and won't be seeing you again. Believe me when I wish you the very best in the future. Stefano.

He'd promised Lanza no scandal would ever touch their marriage and he'd meant it.

Once he'd pressed Send, he read through

the messages from the managers of his other mines and answered where he needed to. The next meeting in Mexico wouldn't come until after his visit to Bulgaria.

When he finally climbed into bed, his mind was on Lanza. He couldn't wait to spend tomorrow with her. It didn't matter what they did because on top of the qualities he'd been discovering about her, her mind intrigued him. That distinction made her stand out from all the other women he'd known.

His last thought before he fell asleep had to do with her and Alberto. If he hadn't died in that crash, he'd be here on his honeymoon with Lanza right now. When Stefano tried to imagine his brother being married to her now, he no longer felt sorry for him. If anything, it was just the opposite…

He must have fallen off because the next thing he knew, Lanza was knocking on his door. "Stefano? Are you awake?" She sounded panicked.

In one bound he was out of bed and pulled

on his robe before running over to the door to open it. She stood there wrapped in a stunning peach-colored robe.

"What's wrong?"

"Fausto's gone! I can't find him. When I went downstairs this morning to see if he needed more water—he'd tipped over the box."

"He has to be around here someplace."

"I've looked everywhere."

"Come on. We'll find him. He couldn't leave the chalet."

Her glorious chestnut hair flounced around her shoulders as they hurried below. The second he flipped on the light at the bottom of the staircase and called out, he heard yapping.

"Fausto?" She'd heard it, too.

Stefano headed for the door to the wood bin where he'd taken out some pieces for the tree stand. He opened it and Fausto sprang out. Laughter burst from him as their little pet darted up the stairs.

At this point she'd started laughing. "Curiosity killed the cat, but not our fox. What do you suppose he came down here for?"

"Since our doors were closed and he was hungry, he probably went on the hunt for food. He must have been shocked when the door closed on him."

"I'll fill his bowls." She started up the stairs.

He followed after her, wanting to put his arms around her and pull her back against him the way he'd done last night. This urge to feel her next to him wasn't going to go away. For the moment the only thing to do was channel his energy with something physical.

While they fixed breakfast and fed the fox, he had an idea. "Have you ever skied?"

"Once in a while."

There were many things Stefano still had to find out about her, but her answer pleased him no end. "As long as the good weather is holding, how would you like to go cross-country skiing with me today?"

"That's something I've never tried. I'd love it!"

She'd answered without thinking about it. That was easy and excited him. "We'll take Fausto to the tree with some food and leave him there while we go exploring."

"I saw that you have a backpack downstairs. I'll make some sandwiches for us so we can be gone as long as we want."

She seemed indefatigable, another trait he welcomed. But more important, she wanted to be with him. That meant everything. "We'll take drinks and a pack of biscotti, too."

"Sounds perfect."

"I'll find an old blanket."

Within a half hour they were ready to go. Her figure did wonders for Carla's ski outfit. She'd fastened her hair at the nape with a band and pulled on the white wool hat that looked sensational on her.

He wrapped the fox in the blanket. When they were ready to take off, he put Fausto under his arm and they headed across the snow toward the forest of trees. Today they saw signs of animal tracks that delighted Lanza.

"Maybe Fausto's family is out here looking for him."

"Why not?" he murmured, willing to humor her.

When they reached the big pine tree, he spread the well-worn blanket on the ground against the trunk and put Fausto down with a pile of food he poured out. "That ought to last him for quite a while."

She lifted concerned blue eyes to Stefano. "I'm almost afraid to leave him, but I know we have to do this for his sake."

"He'll be fine. But if he's unwilling to leave us, we'll take him to a wildlife shelter after we get to the city so he'll survive."

"That will be the right thing to do."

"For the time being, let's stop worrying about him and blaze a new trail. You never know what we might find on our trek today."

CHAPTER NINE

FOR LANZA IT was enough to be out in nature and bask in a white, sunlit world with Stefano. Her love for him was brimming to the surface. It was the kind of love you never got over.

There was no one like him. Since the moment she'd taken vows with him in the cathedral, she'd felt a stirring that had grown into white-hot heat. Being at his fabulous chalet, perched on a mountain as beautiful as this, was her idea of heaven. She couldn't help staring at him. Stefano was a gorgeous man. When he smiled, Lanza was left breathless.

At this high altitude she felt light-headed just looking into those dark eyes that seemed to swallow her alive. Last night he'd kissed her into a new realm of existence. Incredible to think she was so happy today when on the morning of her marriage, it had felt like the end of the world.

Being married to him opened her up to a world of intimacy. Every day with Stefano was turning into an adventure. Lanza hadn't had brothers and had never lived around a man. It made her realize what a sheltered life she'd led as a betrothed royal princess with two sisters and a doting mother. The duties of her father running the country didn't allow a lot of quality time with him.

Today she was so excited to be alive, she wanted to shout it to the world. But it might set off another avalanche. Being up here she was able to put the princess part of herself away and just be Stefano's wife and soon… his lover. She was living for that.

He put on his ski goggles and they started off in another direction. She used her ski poles to swoosh herself along. His long, powerful legs meant she had to work harder to keep up, but it was fun. He had great legs.

"Thank you for not taking us to the Caribbean. Being here is a dream vacation for me. Obviously, you never intended to take us there. I love it that no one knows where we are."

He eyed her through the amber lenses. "I didn't want to have to fly clear across the world after our marathon wedding day."

"With all the travel you do, it doesn't surprise me you would dread a long flight that had nothing to do with business. I was dreading it like the plague."

She thought she heard a chuckle. "You don't enjoy a beach vacation?"

"They're all right, but in my mind you need to be with your soul mate to enjoy a tropical setting."

"You sound like a true romantic."

Lanza nodded. "That's what comes from reading romantic fiction at a very young age."

"You're talking *Pride and Prejudice*?"

"One of them."

"I guess I'm going to have to read it."

She laughed. "You might like it."

He slowed his pace. "Did you bring a copy with you?"

"No. While I was preparing for our wedding, I packed that book and others in a box with a few childhood treasures. What about you?"

"My childhood things are still in my bedroom at the palace."

"I envy you to have been given your freedom for as long as it lasted. To think you had this chalet where you could escape! You've been a very lucky man."

There was a pause before he spoke again. "I felt sorry for you the moment you agreed to be my wife. I'm a poor substitute for my outstanding brother, who was already prepared to be a devoted husband."

Except she'd never loved Alberto, had never desired him or wanted to feel his mouth on hers. Stefano could have no idea how she longed to lie with him all night, knowing his kisses and caresses. Just thinking about being in his arms made her shiver with excitement. Maybe tonight.

"I'm afraid that experience wasn't meant to be. But I do realize his death was tragic when I know you two were so close. How terribly you must miss him. Losing him brought changes to all our lives, turning our worlds upside down."

"That they were," he muttered.

"Odd, isn't it, that in surrendering your freedom, you've given me mine? Even though I'm a royal and always will be, for the first time I feel free with a husband like you. I love your rules of engagement that are giving us time to get to know each other."

Except that in her heart of hearts, she had real feelings for her new husband and wanted him to love her. She couldn't bear the thought that after they got home, he would leave on business without her.

His dark brows furrowed. "More and more I regret the harshness of that message I had sent to you."

"Let's forget that. My father wasn't kidding when he told me I wouldn't regret marrying you. He was right."

In that regard, her father *had* been right. Overnight she'd fallen for Stefano, who had no idea how her heart was aching to win his love.

On that note she took off, wanting to beat him to a tree-lined ridge she could see in the distance. With his athleticism, he could overtake her in seconds, but curiously enough he took his time and reached the ridge long after she'd arrived to view the next breathtaking range of mountains beyond.

She turned to him. "Would you mind opening the backpack? I'm hungry for a sandwich and some water."

"The way you move so fast burning energy, that doesn't surprise me. When I think back on my friends who do cross country with me, I'm sure they would have trouble keeping up with you."

"This has been the exercise I've needed. But considering your expertise at sports, I would imagine your friends are no different and could outski anyone."

"Enzo is the real pro."

Stefano was modest, too. He removed the pack from his shoulders and opened the flap so she could pull out what she wanted. Lanza noticed he was hungry, too. She relished this moment with him as they ate their fill and finished off their meal with some biscotti.

"Mmm, that tasted good."

Stefano looked around. "We've come a long way and the afternoon wind has started to pick up. It might be smart to head back."

She squinted at him. "You wouldn't be worried about Fausto?" she teased.

"Would you be surprised if I admitted I was?"

Lanza put her empty water bottle back in the pack. "Like I told you a little while ago, I don't regret marrying you and this is one of the reasons why."

"I'll take that as a compliment."

"You should. Not everyone would care that a larger predator could come along and snatch him for prey." There was a goodness and tenderness in Stefano that made her love him all the more.

"We'll have to hope the last dumpling I fed him last night has made him strong enough to ward off his enemies."

She laughed. "You gave him one?" When he told her things like that, she was touched by his words, but tried to hide it.

"You never saw anything disappear so fast. He has good taste."

Stop, Stefano. Every word and gesture enamored her. Already it was killing her that he planned to live part of his life away from her when he left for his various mines. "When you're starving, any morsel will do. By the way, what kind of meat do you have in the freezer?"

"As I recall, there are several salmon steaks and a couple of lamb roasts."

"What sounds best to you and I'll fix it for dinner."

"Whatever is easiest."

She smiled. "The steaks will thaw faster. That settles it. Now I'm ready to take off and have to admit I'd like to find out what Fausto has been up to all day."

"First, I want this." He wrapped her in his arms and gave her a long, hungry kiss that robbed her of breath. Finally, he let her go. "You taste so good I never want to stop."

His words caused her to blush before they started across the snow, avoiding their old tracks. It took less energy to make new ones. They spotted some chamois and watched a golden eagle make its way to a peak. Eventually, they reached their destination and skied in through the trees to the one where they'd first found the dying fox.

The sight of the blanket with no food and no Fausto caused her spirits to plummet. "It looks like our plan worked," she murmured, trying to keep the disappointment out of her voice.

"That blanket should have been thrown out long ago. We'll leave it here."

Lanza felt tears sting her eyelids. "He won't be back, which is the way it should be." She shoved on, not wanting to dwell on where he was or what might have happened to him. There'd been no sign of a struggle or blood. That was a good thing.

They kept going without looking back. She hated that this day was almost over. The joy of skiing with Stefano, of watching and loving him in this private world, was almost too much for her. Though the sun was close to falling behind the mountains, she wasn't ready to call it a day. She'd never forget today, but her legs would pay the price in the morning for trying to keep up with him.

Once they reached the chalet, she undid her skis and carried them inside with the poles. Next, she got out of her ski clothes and removed her hat, putting them in the closet. Not waiting for Stefano, she hurried up the stairs to her bedroom. Though she was worried about the fox, her mind and heart were centered on Stefano and how he made her feel.

A hot shower was exactly what she needed; after which she dressed in black wool pants and a tan pullover. Later tonight she'd wash and dry her hair, but right now she needed to thaw the fish in the microwave and get the pasta started for their dinner. He would be hungry and she was eager to fix food he liked. She'd seen boxes of fettuccine noodles on the shelf.

On her way to the kitchen, she stopped in her tracks to glimpse Stefano hunkered down by the box in front of the fireplace he'd turned on...*feeding Fausto*!

"What on earth...?" She rushed over and knelt down next to him.

"Our little fox followed us home. I was just walking inside the chalet with my gear when I heard yipping and saw him coming running toward me."

"All the way across in the deep snow? I don't believe it!"

"I let him inside and brought up the box."

This time the tears overflowed her lashes. "Oh, Stefano—"

Before she could take another breath, he slid an arm around her shoulders and looked into her eyes with an expression she hadn't seen before, suffusing her with heat. "Somehow he knows he's loved."

Before she realized what was happening, Stefano's dark head descended and he covered her mouth with his own the way she'd been aching for all day. This kiss was transforming her.

Suddenly, he was coaxing her mouth open to take their kiss deeper and longer. The divine sensation stopped her from thinking. She went where he led, never wanting him to stop.

Alberto had kissed her each time he'd been with her, but it was nothing like this. With all the reading she'd done, all the films she'd seen and accounts she'd heard from friends, nothing in this world had prepared her for the experience of being kissed by her exciting husband.

Little did he know he was changing her whole world as he pulled her so close she could hardly breathe. Helpless against such pleasure, she slid her hands up his chest and around his neck.

His hands roaming over her back and hips lit a fire inside her. It was real and not a part of her imagination. Anything she'd felt with Alberto bore no resemblance to the rapture Stefano was creating with the slightest touch of his hands and mouth. His enticing scent and the slight rasp of his dark beard against her skin drove her growing desire for him to a wild pitch.

The sensual part of her nature had come alive in his arms and she didn't want to bring it to an end. Lanza was embarrassed for being such a vulnerable mark. It bothered her that the virginal princess was easier prey than Fausto would ever have been *if* he hadn't followed them back to the chalet before dark because he sensed danger.

The way Stefano kissed and held her, she was reeling out of control. Her wholehearted response to his lovemaking meant that he could be in no doubt what he was doing to her. She cried out his name as her body throbbed with desire for him.

But at that moment he unexpectedly relinquished her mouth and put her away from him in a gentle gesture. It produced a protesting moan from her.

"I'm sorry for crossing a line with you, Lanza," he murmured and got to his feet.

"But you didn't." She rose to her feet. "I could have stopped it and you know it."

He shook his head. "The thing is, I made a promise to help you get comfortable with me first."

"Can't you tell that's what's happening?"

"I don't want you to think I'm taking advantage of you. I don't want to make any more mistakes with you like I did in the beginning."

How ironic that she was learning how to do what he did and live in the moment. In fact, that was what she intended to do until they left the chalet. For now she would pretend Stefano could really love her as she loved him. Once they were back in the real world, she feared all would be different.

Lanza stood up and went into the kitchen to start dinner. Stefano took the fox downstairs. When he came back up, he undid a package marked salmon he put in the microwave to thaw. "I'll freshen up and be back."

While he was gone, she set the table with wine and candles, and made some bruschetta for an appetizer. When she noticed he'd come back to the living room freshly shaven, she turned on the grill and cooked the salmon. The steaks only took a few minutes. Finally, everything was ready including the coffee.

"La cena è pronta, Stefano," she called to him.

"Meraviglioso." He came into the kitchen and took their laden plates to the table without glancing at her.

She followed with the tray of coffee and cups, drinking in how incredibly appealing he was, wearing navy trousers and a white pullover. No man in Domodossola or

Umbriano could measure up to him, not in looks or charisma.

Tonight was like déjà vu, but instead of dumplings, he wolfed down the bruschetta so fast she had to bring more to the table. He lifted his head. "You could open a restaurant, Lanza. Do you know that?"

"That's been a dream of mine for a while."

He'd already made inroads into the fettuccine and salmon. "How so?"

"Recently, I've urged father to have a soup kitchen constructed in the western part of the city next to the new housing for the homeless and immigrants. He thinks it's a good idea, but there are other needs that have more priority. It's a case of raising more money."

She smiled at him. "Perhaps because you're his new son-in-law, you could talk him into allocating some funds as an experiment. Maybe match them with donations from some of our wealthier citizens. I'd love to at least get it started and run it until I can find volunteers who'll be happy to work there full-time. Many people everywhere would help if given the opportunity."

He stared at her in surprise. "You'd really like to take on that kind of responsibility?"

"A soup kitchen is only one of my interests."

Stefano put down his fork. "What else?"

She was flattered by his interest and plunged away. "I told you about Duccio, who taught me how to play cards. He, like so many of the disabled naval veterans still do, needed housing and better health care. They've fought for our country and we have a moral obligation to pay them back."

"Alberto never told me you were a philanthropist at heart."

She sipped her coffee. "Don't assume I'm a Mother Teresa–type with a list of a dozen causes that are underfunded and don't have the right people with organizational skills. But you can't live in this world without seeing problems. I would hope that's true, even if I'm a royal."

"So what *did* you and my brother talk about if it wasn't about the needs of the people?"

"Between elaborate breakfasts, lunches and dinners, we rowed on the lake out in back of the palace and went horseback riding. Our conversation centered mostly on his duties for your father and my schooling.

"We both agreed we got annoyed with our tutors. Instead of learning Latin and studying the Punic Wars, we would have much preferred to get into the latest inroads in technology and become computer savvy. He once told me that if he'd been granted one wish, he would have become a space scientist."

That brought a sad expression to Stefano's face. "I remember when he was given a telescope that was set up in his room. He'd look through it all the time and should have been allowed to pursue his studies in science."

She swallowed hard to hear his pain. "Now he's in heaven, where he's learning amazing things."

"I'd like to believe that."

Lanza eyed him directly. "Don't you believe in an afterlife?"

"Do you?" He turned the question on her.

She wondered if her answer was important to him, wishing it didn't matter. "Definitely. This beautiful world wouldn't have been created only for everything to end once we'd lived out our lives here. After what we learn, it wouldn't make sense not to take that knowledge to the next world."

As he'd been thinking ever since he'd married Lanza, Stefano thought she was the most intriguing female he'd ever met in his life. There were so many parts that made up the whole of her; he knew he hadn't even skimmed the surface.

After holding her in his arms and kissing her earlier, he also discovered she was the most desirable woman he'd ever been with, and he'd been with a lot of them over the years. His heart still hadn't recovered from the shock since her mouth had opened to the pressure of his. Her response had shaken him to the foundation.

The two of them had experienced an overwhelming surge of passion earlier that had been real. But he shouldn't have acted on his desire this soon when he'd told her they'd give their marriage time until she was ready for intimacy. The chemistry between them had made it almost impossible for him to let her go.

Following that thought came a sensation of guilt when he realized that his own brother would have been the one to make love to her if he hadn't died. He closed his eyes tightly. What he needed to do was shut off those thoughts.

With a sharp intake of breath he said, "After that fabulous meal, I'm going to do the dishes while you relax. When I've finished, are you up for another game of cards before we go to bed?"

"Yes."

He eyed her in amusement. "I was thinking of playing Briscola. Let's play for higher stakes."

"You're on." Her eyes glowed like gems.

Stefano's mind went back to the planning stage of this supposedly quick trip to the mountains. After two days his intention had been to take her on a sterile drive to the Mediterranean while they made desultory talk trying to get to know each other.

Not in his wildest dreams would he have imagined being snowed in with Lanza enjoying a domestic scene like this with a wife who thrilled him. Eager to join her, he finished up in record time, but when he went to get the cards, he saw that she'd already taken them from the breakfront and was looking at the back side of one.

"What's caught your eye?" He sat down next to her.

"The drawings of clubs and swords. And of course *denari* for gambling. But I guess that's not unusual considering it was the warriors who passed time playing cards until their next war."

Everything she said was unexpected and kept him fascinated. "What would you have drawn?"

"I have no talent, but my sister Fausta does. She would probably have designed the heads of dogs and birds. She's a wonderful artist and could sell her work." Lanza looked up at him. "If you're ready, I'll deal." The glint in her eye told him she was prepared to do battle and would give him no quarter.

At the end of three rounds, he'd won the first two, but she won the last one. "Bravo, Lanza. Let's go another round."

"I'm in, but I swear you're better at this than I am. Do you play cards a lot during your downtime at the mining camps?"

"Hardly ever. Mostly I eat and sleep after putting in twenty hours work a day."

"Do the wives join their husbands at the camps? I'm talking about your managers."

"No. There'd be nothing for the women to do."

"Does that mean you would never take me with you?"

He stared hard at her. "I can promise you wouldn't be happy. It's not a place to be if you don't have a job there."

"Could you give me one? I enjoyed learning about the things you told me in your emails. Your work is so important I'd like to be a part of it if I could. At night we could be together whether it's in a tent or sleeping in the out of doors. The six weeks you have to be gone on your various trips wouldn't matter if we were together."

Stefano couldn't believe what he was hearing. "What if you became pregnant?"

"Then I'd travel with you until I couldn't."

"Your family wouldn't approve."

"But you're my husband. I vowed to honor *you*."

Perhaps it could work since his wife wanted her freedom. All along she'd maintained that was what she craved. With Stefano's influence, his new father-in-law might not be averse to Lanza traveling with him once in a while.

To have his wife at the mines and go to bed with her every night would be heaven for him. But he'd have to figure out a job she could do. It was something to think about.

They played another round, and she won. "Now that I'm the winner, will you promise to figure out a job for me to do when you have to leave for your next mine visit?"

"That will be in Argentina."

"Hmm. I've never been there, but I've studied Spanish with my language tutor."

"I promise to see what I can do."

She got up from the floor. "It's been a wonderful day. I'm going to say good-night and hope you get a good sleep."

Stefano didn't want her to go to bed yet, but after he'd brought a halt to their love-making, what did he expect? He sat there in shock while she left the living room.

The thought of her traveling with him and having his baby was exciting to him. If any woman was meant to have children it was Lanza. He knew she wanted him. He had proof of that in the way she'd clung to him. Otherwise, she would have pushed him away and run to her bedroom the second he'd put his arm around her.

In hindsight Stefano recognized that a part of him had put off marrying anyone and having children because he hadn't met Lanza yet. But there was more to it. Deep inside he'd known he couldn't escape the fact that he'd been born royal. Bringing a child into the world wouldn't exempt it from being titled, no matter how he much he wished it otherwise. But he didn't feel that way any longer.

Their marriage had already made a big change in him. The more he thought about it, the more he admitted what a coward he'd been. For the first time in his life he felt shame at what he'd done by running away. He'd left it to Alberto and his sister to carry on. To his chagrin, his actions had resulted in unintended consequences.

Lanza honestly hadn't believed he'd

wanted children. How could she when he'd made it clear they would be living separate lives when he wasn't helping her father? By promising her fidelity to him, she'd set herself up to exist in a childless marriage. How selfish was that!

He'd hurt her in ways he'd hadn't dreamed of and now he had a huge problem to repair. As he got ready for bed, Stefano realized this was going to take time to fix, including figuring out a job she could do if she went with him on his trips. So far he'd practically kissed her into oblivion and was already aching to get her in his arms again.

After a restless night, he got up early, took Fausto outside where he could eat and play, then made a big breakfast. Not wanting to knock on her door when she didn't come to the dining room, he phoned her.

"Are you up? I've made breakfast."

"I just washed my hair and am drying it." All that glorious hair… "I can't come for a half hour."

"Fine. I'll keep it warm for us."

"Thank you."

While he waited, he walked back to his bedroom and got on the computer. He spotted Enzo's email first.

Hi, Stefano. Electricity will be restored by the end of the day. No news yet on the road opening. Hope you two are all right.

Stefano smiled to himself. They were more than all right.

He knew what his friend was really asking. The last time the two of them had gotten into a serious talk, Enzo knew Stefano was dying inside over having to marry his brother's fiancée.

In fact, he'd been dreading it and couldn't face a vacation in the sand and sun with a woman he could never love. He and Lanza had been on the same wavelength about a beach vacation being the place if you were in love.

He'd brought her to the chalet because it had been his wedding present to Alberto, but he hadn't believed she would like it here.

With the diversion of a driving tour, they'd somehow be able to get through the two weeks of *ennui*.

It was incredible how wrong he'd been about everything. Nothing was as he'd assumed or imagined.

You're a great friend. It's all good news, amico. Thanks for keeping me posted. S.

No doubt Enzo would be in shock when he received this email. One day soon Stefano would confide in him about the true state of his feelings over his marriage.

He pressed Send and moved on to the next message. Farther down he saw a return message from Alicia Montoya.

Tell me it isn't true that you're married, Stefano. I asked the head boss. He said it was, but nothing else. I don't understand.

Stefano had kept his royal identity a secret all these years except from his head mining engineers. Unfortunately, Alicia couldn't let this go.

Alicia, I am married to a woman I met very recently. It was sudden and I'm happy. I hope in time you will be, too.

He wouldn't respond to her again.

Once that was sent, he checked his other messages before going back to the living room. Lanza had gone to the kitchen to take their plates out of the oven. She was wearing a pair of tan pants and a print blouse.

Stefano couldn't take his eyes off her figure or her hair. She'd put it in a becoming braid that made her look younger than her twenty-three years. Whether on top of her head, flowing over her shoulders or fixed like this, she was a vision.

He took one of the plates from her. "How did you sleep?"

Her eyes swerved to his. "Too well." They walked to the dining room table and sat down. "I awakened with aches and pains from our workout yesterday and the day before. Today I'm going to lie near the fire and read."

"Sounds good. After we eat, I need to make some repairs around the chalet. The wind loosened some of the shutters and there's a basement window that needs fixing." They tucked into the scrambled eggs and sausage he'd cooked. He was glad to see her appetite hadn't suffered.

"Where's Fausto?"

"Outside somewhere."

"Was he still in his box this morning?"

Stefano nodded. "I think he learned his lesson about staying put so he wouldn't get trapped again."

"He's a little rascal."

"I agree. By the way, Enzo wrote. We're supposed to get electricity by this evening."

"Yes. I heard as much on the radio a little while ago, but they still haven't cleared the road covered by that avalanche."

"Lanza, if you're anxious to leave, Enzo will have a helicopter sent for us."

"Oh, no!" she cried immediately. "I mean… That is…unless you've grown restless."

That little outburst was worth its weight in gold to Stefano. There was the proof that she loved it here as much as he did. It revealed another truth to him. This intimate time with his enticing wife had grown on him to the point that he didn't want to budge from his favorite spot.

CHAPTER TEN

LANZA NEVER WANTED to leave the mountains and was embarrassed to have reacted so strongly. The longer they stayed away from everyone, the happier she would be. Once they were back at the palace, the world would descend on them. While they were here, she had Stefano to herself.

She feared he could never love her the way she loved him. But she cherished the fact that this would probably be the only time in her life when they would have this kind of privacy. It was incredible that no one knew where they were except Enzo. If they were trapped here for a month, she'd love it.

After clearing the table, she went back to the bedroom for her spy novel and came out to the living room once more to lie on the couch and finish the book. Her only problem was her inability to concentrate. Snatches of earlier conversations sent her down one road after another, each tidbit of information giving her insight into his character.

Out of the corner of her eye she saw their Christmas tree, the one he'd brought home for her when he didn't have to. Fausto's blanket still sat in front of the fireplace. Stefano had made the box into a home for the fox with bowls of food and water. It was right there that he'd kissed her close to senseless. Her body still throbbed from the sensations that had sent her spiraling to a different universe.

Love's first kiss, the famous line delivered in angry mockery from the lips of the evil queen in a certain childhood fairy tale, had taken on new meaning for her. She'd never get over what his hands and mouth had done to her. The feel of his hard body was a revelation. Lanza had been transformed into a different person. That was Stefano's doing.

By midafternoon Lanza grew restless and got up from the couch. She would have to finish the story another time. The Vacherin and Gruyère cheeses in the fridge had been calling to her. She could make up a pot of *fondue au fromage.* They could eat it with one of the loaves of French bread from the freezer.

Stefano had been outside a long time and no doubt was hungry. His supply of wines included Kirsch cherry wine, a perfect one to add flavor. She got busy grating cheese and hurried downstairs to the freezer so the bread could thaw in time for dinner.

Lanza had always enjoyed cooking, but had never cooked on a regular basis in her life until now. Of course, even if she couldn't boil water, that wouldn't have bothered Stefano. He knew how to cook and had been fending for himself for years. But it made her happy she could do her part while they were cut off from the world for a little while. She adored him and couldn't do enough for him.

Before long he came in for a drink of

water, bringing a draft of cold air with him. "Um, that fondue looks good enough to eat."

She laughed. "Let's hope. It's ready when you are. Did you get all the chores done?"

"Yup. I'll freshen up and be right back."

While he was gone she set the table with the fondue forks and put on a bottle of white wine to go with their meal. By the time he returned, she'd brought the pot of bubbly yellow fondue to the table.

"Food for a king!" Stefano exclaimed, his dark eyes shining with excitement as he sat down.

"That's what you will be one of these days, or have you forgotten?"

"I'm trying," he said under his breath, but she heard him and couldn't believe she'd said it when she knew how hard he'd fought to be a nonroyal.

"I'm sorry, Stefano. I wasn't thinking when I said that."

"I shouldn't have said what I did, either." His apology meant a lot. "How did you know this is my favorite dish after being outside in the snow all day?"

"It's mine, too. Who stocked all your shelves and freezer for you?"

"I have a housekeeper, Angelina, who lives in the city. When I asked her to do some shopping for me because I was bringing my bride to the chalet for our honeymoon, she told me to leave it to her."

"You found yourself a real treasure."

"She's been with me for five years."

"I hope you give her a big bonus for supplying us with so much food. She couldn't have known about the avalanche."

"She goes overboard when she finds out I'm coming with my friends. This time she wanted to make it special for you."

"We've been blessed."

His eyes held hers for a moment. "I'll tell her what you said. It will mean the world to her." That brought a lump to her throat.

He started inhaling his dinner. "This fondue is divine."

"At the rate you're going, I'll have to make another pot."

She waited for him to say, "Would you?" But to her surprise he said, "I'll make the next batch. It won't be as good as yours."

Unbelievably, he did get up after he'd finished off the food and started making another meal.

"While you do that, I'll go downstairs and see if Fausto is ready to come in."

"He was gone all day, but I'm sure he's back now. It's dark out and the temperature dropped this afternoon. There might be another storm, but not like the last one."

With the cozy atmosphere inside the chalet, Lanza hoped it was a big blizzard. She went down and turned on the light. To test if the electricity had come on, she turned off the generator. Sure enough there was a flicker, but the lights stayed on. Stefano would be pleased.

Next, she went over to the door and opened it. "Fausto?" He must have been waiting because he bounded inside and crawled inside his box. What a change from the day they'd found him barely alive.

"Wherever he's been, he was ready to come home," she announced at the top of the stairs. "And guess what? The electricity did come on, so I turned off the generator."

"That's good news. Enzo and his wife will be pleased, because they've had to use their generator, too. But if I know my friend, he's made the best of it and they're enjoying it."

Lanza imagined they did since they'd only been married a few months. Her stomach clenched. Because Stefano had been forced to marry her, it meant he wouldn't be able to see Enzo or his other friends nearly as often as before. Besides the royal duties that would infringe on his business interests, he would now be living in Domodossola and forced to give up an enormous part of his former life.

Life hadn't been fair to either of them.

Lanza had been forced to marry another man. After Alberto had died, she'd assumed she'd be free to make a new life for herself, but her parents had insisted that the New Year Wedding would take place. She knew her father's health wasn't good, but they could have insisted that one of her sisters get married to one of the available princes on their short list. It didn't have to be Stefano.

No one except her aunt had ever considered how she'd really felt about her betrothal to Alberto, or how close she'd come to running away and never returning. Only Ottavia's promise that one day she'd find a man she could love had helped her to survive this long.

Ironically, her words had been prophetic and Lanza found herself deeply in love with the man she'd married. Her eyes watered. If he could never return her love…

Lanza started doing the dishes, but she was all stirred up inside. So much for living out her fantasy with Stefano while they were alone. If she went on playing that delusional game, it would be to her detriment.

"Stefano?" Lanza walked into the dining

room. "I'm going to say good-night so I can finish my book. See you in the morning."

His head shot up. "You can't go yet. I've got Scrabble all set up for us."

Her spirits lifted immediately. He wanted to be with her. "Then watch out. I'm a good speller."

They played until late. He walked around the table and squeezed her shoulders. "I love being with you no matter what we do." She got up from the chair and turned into his arms. His kiss didn't last long enough. He'd said he wanted to go slowly, but that was ridiculous when she was on fire for him. Somehow she needed to find a way to speed things up.

Taking the initiative, she cupped his face. "Get a good sleep, Stefano." She said it with a smile before heading to her bedroom. From here on out she would do what she could to entice him until he realized she was so comfortable, she wanted to climb into his bed and stay there.

For the next three days they kept Fausto

fed and cooked breakfast together. She'd done a wash of her clothes and the fox's blanket. Lanza adored going cross-country skiing and got quite good at it. She relished every minute with him.

They did three different exciting trails where they saw all kinds of wildlife, including a moose. Their strenuous ski adventures wore her out. Sometimes they raced each other, but he always won and they ended up kissing each other beneath a glorious sun. His sensuous smile melted her bones, leaving her limp with longing.

Every time they returned to the chalet, they'd make a sandwich, then lie on the floor in front of the fire and listen to music from his radio. He'd start to kiss her and she'd kiss him back, but he never tried to do anything more. She ended up taking long, hot showers, then getting into bed with the novels she'd brought.

After a week had gone by, they had news. When she appeared in the kitchen to fix breakfast dressed in wool pants and a cherry-red sweater, Stefano was waiting for her in trousers and a tan sport shirt. The sight of him always made her breath catch, but there was a different aura about him this morning.

"We have phone service."

No.

"Enzo called me a minute ago and the snow has been cleared from the mountain road enough for him to make it up here. He'll be bringing my car." Stefano sounded so happy, her heart plunged to her feet.

She reached for an apple. Their supply had grown low. "How soon are you expecting him so I can start packing?"

He rubbed the front of his chest in an absent gesture. "I was waiting to talk it over with you. Do you want to take the driving tour I'd planned for us?"

Lanza had to suppress a moan. "I'll do whatever you'd like." Did he want to leave? She couldn't bear it.

His dark eyes narrowed on her features. "We'll take Fausto with us when we drop

Enzo back at his office. Then I'll drive you to one of my favorite restaurants for a big lunch and we'll talk about plans."

"Does this mean you'll be assigning security for us?" She dreaded the idea of it. Here they'd been free of everything and everyone. "I guess you'll have to because people will recognize us. Our secret will be out."

"Not if we disguise ourselves in our ski outfits and sunglasses. We'll look like typical tourists. On our way out of the city we'll leave our little fox at the wildlife shelter. I'll make a donation so they'll look after him."

That last comment told her he'd gotten attached to Fausto, but she still felt ill. This was the end of her idyll, the happiest time she'd ever had in her life, all because of Stefano. With the opening of the road, this whole glorious time had come to an end.

"Go ahead and call Enzo back. I'll get started packing."

With a heart so heavy she wanted to die, Lanza hurried to the bedroom and began putting things in her suitcase. It didn't take long since she hadn't worn the clothes meant for the tropics. Once she'd packed her cosmetics, she was ready.

An hour later, after making the bed, she put her hair in a braid. No one would recognize her wearing her hair like that. She slipped on Carla's ski outfit and carried her cases to the stairs. Lanza found Stefano in the kitchen making coffee. He handed her a mug to drink.

"I'll take the box downstairs to load in the car."

Lanza followed with her cases. He must have already taken his down. She couldn't look at the Christmas tree in the corner of the living room. It hurt too terribly. She was in excruciating pain when she remembered the thrilling moments in here they'd shared, especially the rapture she'd experienced in his arms. Sobs welled in her throat. Somehow she had to find a way to stifle them.

Enzo's voice carried as she reached the door entrance. The two men sounded thrilled to see each other. She opened it into the sunlight and walked out to the car, glad for her sunglasses.

"Buon giorno, Enzo," she called to him. Today he appeared without a ski hat and was dressed in a suit and tie. Stefano had told her they'd be driving him to the bank."

"Lanza—" He hurried around the car toward her. "I hope you don't mind my calling you that."

"I want you to."

He smiled. "It's good to see you again, but I have to admit I wouldn't have recognized you in that outfit."

"Or my braid?" she teased.

"Exactly." His blue eyes played over her with even more masculine interest than before. "I'm sorry you had to wait so long to be rescued."

"Since you've stayed at this chalet many, many times, then you know how comfortable we've been. We appreciate your coming."

"It's my pleasure, believe me." Stefano had already put the box on the back seat of the car. No man on the planet could look as jaw-droppingly handsome as her husband in his ski clothes and sunglasses. She opened the car door and got in next to it.

Her husband walked over to her. "I'd like you to ride in front with me."

He didn't need to keep up the pretense in front of his friend. She fastened her seat belt. "If you don't mind, I'd like to be by Fausto until we have to say goodbye to him. Will that be all right?"

Lanza heard him take in a quick breath. "Of course." He shut the door and put their luggage in the back end of the vehicle. Then he slid behind the wheel.

Enzo got in the front passenger seat, and they made their way out to the mountain road, using the remote to open the gate for them. It was astounding how much snow had fallen the night of the blizzard.

She couldn't break down sobbing, but she wanted to. Instead, she looked inside the box at Fausto, who had no idea what was going on. He had to be anxious. "We're taking you to a place where you'll be safe and cared for, but I'm going to miss you."

Enzo wanted to know all about him and directed his questions to her while Stefano maneuvered their car through so much snow she didn't know how they would make it.

She gasped when they reached the avalanche area. It had been a massive slide. A dozen men and vehicles were working to clear the road completely. Once they got past everything, the snow wasn't quite as deep and it only took them a half hour to drive on snow-packed roads to the main city of Umbriano, the same name as the country.

Stefano drove him to the city center and drew up in front of the bank where Enzo worked. He leaned over to press her hand. "My wife and I hope to see you soon." Then he turned to Stefano and the two men hugged before he got out of the car. "Talk to you later." He flashed them both a big smile and hurried inside the building.

Before Stefano pulled out into traffic, he looked over his shoulder at her. "I think we'll drop off Fausto first. Then we can take all the time we want to eat."

"Bene" was all she could get out at the moment.

Five minutes later he drove into the parking lot in front of a building attached to a spacious preserve on the edge of the woods. The sign said *Rifugio Faunistico di Umbriano.*

She felt a pain in the pit of her stomach as Stefano got out and opened the back door to get the box. His face was taut with emotion, mirroring her anxiety that the fox was going to face a whole new life. But her thoughts had gone far beyond Fausto. She was already in mourning that this precious time with Stefano was coming to an end. If only he knew how much she loved him…

Lanza slid out her side and held the door open for him so he could carry the box inside. The reception room had a long counter with a man in glasses and a lab coat working behind it. Stefano put the box down and explained why they'd come.

"Cute little fellow. Where did you find

him?" So far the man hadn't recognized them or he would have addressed Stefano as *Your Highness.* That was a good sign.

"On Monte Viso, above the area of the avalanche, right after the storm."

"He was close to death," Lanza asserted. "After we fed him and he recovered, we took him back to the exact place where we'd found him, but he refused to run away."

"He got a taste of your food. That's natural."

"Can you introduce him back into the wild?"

The older man nodded. "That's our job. We'll do everything possible."

Stefano slipped him some euros. "My wife and I will be interested to know how he does and make inquiries."

"Of course."

"His name is Fausto," Lanza blurted. Just saying the name caused the fox to lift its head.

The worker laughed. "He has a name already?"

"My wife is very attached to him."

"I can see that, but he wouldn't make the most satisfactory pet. Not like a dog or a cat."

"I know."

"You brought him to the right place. We'll do all we can."

"Bless you," she murmured before running outside to the car. In a few minutes Stefano followed in time to shut her door. By the time he'd gone around to the driver's side, she'd broken down in tears. While her face was buried in her hands, she felt Stefano's arm go around her and pull her against him.

He kissed the side of her face and hair. "I know exactly how you feel. As I told the man, we'll call in a few days and find out how he's getting on."

"Thank you." Shaken by his tenderness, she wiped the tears with the backs of her hands and moved out of his arms though she'd wanted to stay in his arms forever.

He started the car, but instead of taking

them to a restaurant, he drove them to a farm. "Why are we coming here?"

"I thought you might enjoy a sleigh ride before we eat."

"You're kidding! How exciting!"

An older man came out of the barn and told them to get in the sleigh pulled by two horses. He'd supplied blankets for their comfort and they took a half hour's journey along the path through the nearby woods.

"What made you think about this?"

"I knew we'd both be upset to have to leave Fausto and thought we might enjoy something different to get our minds off him."

Her heart pounded in her chest. "This is a wonderful surprise. I love it. Thank you, Stefano." Every minute with him brought new thrills and bonded her to him.

When it came to an end and they'd thanked the farmer, he drove them to Ristorante Alasso, an elegant restaurant that served the best burrata antipasto she'd ever eaten. The shell of mozzarella contained a semisoft white Italian cheese made with cream and was to-die-for. Delicious ravioli followed with a dessert of cappuccino and cannoli.

Stefano smiled at her after she took her last bite. "Feel better?"

"What a question. This was a superb meal."

"But it hasn't taken the sadness from your eyes."

"Nor yours, but I have an idea. If you'll take me to the airport now, I'll fly to Rome to visit my aunt. That will leave you free to be gone for a week. I'll fly to Domodossola Airport when you return and we'll take a limo to the palace together."

Stefano leaned forward and eyed her intently. "I'm going to be honest with you. There's no place on earth I'd rather be than the chalet. If it hadn't been for Fausto, who needs attention, I would have told Enzo not to come for us until we had to leave at the end of our two weeks.

"Are you serious?" she cried, so overjoyed she couldn't find words.

"We haven't even gone skiing yet and the Monte Viso resort is a mere twenty minutes away. This kind of snow calls to you, but maybe you've had enough of it."

He was begging to go back!

She felt it in every atom of her body. In fact, she was almost sick with excitement at the prospect of being isolated with him for another week. Anything could happen now.

"I'd much rather ski than travel around the Mediterranean," she stated. "On our way back to the chalet, why don't we pick up fresh salad and some pastries to last us for another week."

"Don't forget chocolate," he added. There was no mistaking the light shining in those dark eyes before he sat back. "Now I can breathe again."

He didn't know the half of it.

She watched him put money on the table before they left to find a store. Another new experience awaited her when she went into a grocery store to shop. Lanza had always wondered what it would be like to do anything as ordinary as walk around a store with the husband you loved.

Being with Stefano was an adventure she loved with every fiber of her being. They laughed while they planned their meals for the week and ended up buying more food than they would need, but he insisted more was much better than less.

To her amazement he bought half a dozen bottles of Almond 22 Pink India Pale Ale. He admitted to developing a taste for it over the years and dared her to try it. In her euphoric mood, there was no way to deny him. "I'll have some tonight."

"While we play some more Scrabble, right? You won't go to bed on me too soon?"

Surely, he was joking. She had no plans to disappear on him. His plea connected to her in a way he wouldn't have believed. "I promise."

"I'm going to hold you to it," he said in his deep voice that wound its way to her insides, turning them to jelly.

After loading the car, they headed for the

turnoff on the outskirts of the city. "Before we go any farther, do you want to check on Fausto?"

"There's nothing I'd love more." Lanza adored him for suggesting it. "But if we did that, we might as well have not taken him to the refuge in the first place."

"Thus speaks my rational other half."

Even to her own ears, her remark had sounded like a nitpicking wife. She never wanted to be that kind of wearisome woman a man couldn't wait to get away from.

Lanza lowered her head. "I'm afraid that didn't come out right. I was thinking of his welfare without realizing you're missing him, too."

He reached over to clasp her hand, instilling her with warmth. "We'll have to stay busy so we don't worry about him. Oh— while I think about it, take a look at the photo on my phone." He pulled out his cell phone. "I took a picture of him for us to remember before I ran after you."

She did his bidding and found an adorable headshot of Fausto. He was looking up from the box.

Stefano... I love you, I love you.

CHAPTER ELEVEN

THAT EVENING STEFANO set their table on a blanket by the fireplace with all kinds of treats. They'd bought pizza they could warm up. He opened two bottles of beer for them before settling down to play Scrabble while they ate.

After an afternoon of skiing, they were comfortably tired. Tonight there was a special glow about Lanza in the firelight. This evening she wore her hair long. He wished she always wore it this way, loose and flowing. The flush on her cheek was new. He hoped her heightened color before she'd started drinking the beer meant she loved being with him, too.

For his part, he was happy in a way hard to articulate. He couldn't think of another place he'd rather be. As for being with a woman, he had all the woman he wanted right here. Day after day his desire for her had been escalating. Though he'd been sexually attracted to other women, he hadn't felt like this. Being with Lanza was different. She excited him on too many other levels and he worried what her true feelings were for him.

He couldn't tell if she was ready to be loved into oblivion. But before the week was out, he intended to show and tell her how much he wanted her. Forget being comfortable together. They were beyond that.

But if, heaven forbid, he learned that she only tolerated him and the sex that was expected—which he couldn't believe—then things would have to change. They would have a long talk about the best way to make her happy. Lanza didn't deserve to live in a cage if that was how she still felt about their marriage.

"How do you like the beer?" She'd just taken her first sip.

Her enticing mouth smiled at him. "I didn't think it would be this delicious."

"You're a good sport."

"I'm telling you the truth. I really liked it. What a surprise."

He studied her out of half-veiled eyes. *She* was the surprise. Watching her ski today and witness how fast she improved with just a few tips was another exciting revelation to him. Stefano realized his wife could do anything and made the most wonderful companion he could ever have dreamed of.

"Are you tired, Lanza?"

"Pleasantly so. I should have told you before now that you outskied everyone on the piste today. Are you sure you weren't on the Umbriano ski team in another life?"

He chuckled. "Would it surprise you to know Alberto had that distinction for a season?"

She got to her feet. "I had no idea, but I believe you could outski anyone."

"You think?" He loved bantering with her. "I know."

She started cleaning up, but he didn't want this night to end. "The dishes will wait."

"I can tell you're tired, too. It's better to do them now before all that beer gets the best of us."

"Slave driver."

"I heard that." Her grin got to him.

He followed her into the kitchen with the items that needed to go in the fridge. While she stood at the sink to load the dishwasher, he wanted her so much he couldn't resist sliding his arms around her waist. In an instant his plan to go slowly and woo her for a few more days had just gone up in smoke.

Stefano pulled her against him. "Do you have any idea how good you feel? How marvelous you smell?" he murmured against her nape, bringing her closer. "I've been wanting to do this all day." He turned her around and saw the startled look in those heavenly blue eyes. "I need to kiss you again before I go mad."

Stefano didn't give her a chance to breathe as he closed his mouth over hers. He was so hungry for her, he was close to devouring her. His lips roved over every beautiful feature before kissing her again and again. When she clung to him like she'd done before, he knew she wanted this. Desire wasn't something you could hide when it was the real thing.

Unable to stop what was happening, he picked her up in his arms and carried her to one of the couches where he lay back and pulled her down. She trembled as he locked her to him, loving the feel of her hands and mouth that were driving him crazy.

The more they kissed and found ways to bring each other pleasure, the more he discovered he couldn't assuage his longing.

"Stefano." She suddenly said his name. To his chagrin, she eased herself away from him before getting to her feet. She was breathing hard.

He sat up. "Have I done something to offend you?"

"It's not that."

"Yes, it is. I'm going too fast."

"No." She shook her head. "I've been enjoying this time with you a great deal more than I thought I would. That's something I hadn't anticipated. But I guess I still need a little more time."

"That's what I was afraid of."

"It isn't that I don't want to make love, Stefano, but this is all happening so fast."

"That's true, but things have changed, or so I thought."

"You know they have." She folded her arms. "Perhaps because you're a man, you can follow through with your natural inclinations when it appeals to you. Obviously, I've had no problem in that regard, either. But we're not in a hurry, are we?"

"Of course not."

She'd just hung him with his own words by reminding him of that terrible message he'd sent to her about no wedding night. But within a very short amount of time, that man had disappeared. He wanted to take it all back and start over. A lance piercing his body couldn't have done more damage and it was his own fault.

On a groan, Stefano got up from the couch.

"We have a lifetime to work everything out. There's one thing I know about you already. I'll always be able to count on your honesty."

Though it was going to take time, Stefano was determined to win her heart. She was a prize beyond all others. Time was all he had now that he was her husband. Hopefully, their marriage would last for the rest of their lives.

"I depend on yours, too," she murmured. "If you'll excuse me, I'm going to bed." She picked up the radio to take with her.

"I'm sure you're tired and bed sounds good to you."

"It does." She started for the hallway.

"We have another exciting day of skiing tomorrow," he reminded her.

"I can't wait," she called over her shoulder. He believed she meant that. So far they'd enjoyed doing everything together whether cooking, tending Fausto, playing cards or talking. Among other things his wife was a natural at sports, and a moment ago she'd been on fire for him, displaying a hunger for him that was thrilling.

There was no way she could turn off those feelings at will any more than he could. But she didn't have that much experience dealing with desire. He had to ease her into making love with him.

Tomorrow they'd eat dinner at the lodge in disguise once they'd had their fill of skiing. He couldn't wait. Afterward, he'd take her into the bar for dancing where he would have a legitimate reason to put his arms around her and feel the mold of her beautiful body close to him.

He put the game away and turned down the fire before heading for his bedroom. Once he'd looked at his emails, he'd take a quick shower and crawl into bed. Alone. But he didn't intend for this state of affairs to last much longer.

Lanza threw herself across the bed and broke down sobbing into her pillow.

Lying in Stefano's arms tonight, relishing

the taste and feel of him, had brought her ecstasy. But she was afraid he didn't love her. The thought that his heart might not be involved had sent a chill through her body and she'd been the one to break it off.

The thought of his making love to her if he wasn't in love the same way she was hurt her so much she couldn't lie there any longer. It would be better to keep her distance from him and not succumb to her own longings. He'd never take her with him to one of his mines, and she'd spend part of her life in pain every time he went away.

Things would get easier once they'd returned to the palace. The difficulty lay in getting through the rest of this week while they were alone. Yet, there was nothing she wanted more in this world than to stay here with him indefinitely.

Lanza decided she had to be out of her mind. Donetta would tell her she was crazy not to live it up the way a man would do, especially with a husband who looked like Stefano. She could hear her sister now. *For-*

*get being in love. There is no such thing.
Enjoy!*

Fausta would have a different take on it.
She would tell her there was no reason why
she couldn't have her own secret lover. It
wasn't natural to be forced to stay in a marriage with no joy. Her sister was right, but
Lanza couldn't see herself being unfaithful,
or even getting interested in another man.
What would be the use? Stefano was in a
class of his own.

At four in the morning Lanza awakened,
shocked to realize she'd never gotten ready
for bed. The wind had picked up during the
night and moaned around the bedroom windows.

She hurried into the bathroom to change
into her nightgown and brush her teeth.
When she got into bed, she turned on the
radio to a music station to blot out the howl-
ing of the wind. There hadn't been a sign of
it during the day, but the weather changed
fast up here in the mountains.

Lanza finally fell asleep again and didn't

get up until ten in the morning. The wind was even stronger than before and the sky had grown dark. That meant another storm was on the way. They wouldn't be able to ski today. She doubted any lifts could run with these gusts.

She scrambled out of bed to get dressed and brush her hair, which she tied back at the nape. Once she'd done her makeup, she headed for the kitchen, hungry for a pastry and some juice. When she opened the fridge, she saw that the leftover pizza was gone, providing Stefano with breakfast. He'd probably gone outside after eating.

Lanza took her food into the living room where he'd turned up the fire and switched on a lamp. Though Stefano had watered their Christmas tree, it didn't look well. She wandered over to the window while she munched. The spectacular view of the mountains never ceased to exhilarate her, especially with the clouds moving in.

Maybe if Stefano didn't have any other plans for today, she could ask him to show her his huge map of the mines and learn what he did. The wealth he brought into his country staggered her.

As she turned to go back to the kitchen, he walked into the living room, dressed in jeans and a pullover with a look of concern on his face. "I'm glad you're up," he said in his deep voice that told her something was wrong. "I was about to waken you."

Her heart pounded. "What is it?"

Lines bracketed his mouth. "I was doing some work on the computer this morning when I received an emergency alert message from my mining manager in Zacatecas, Mexico. There was a cave-in at the Casale mine that has trapped some miners. I have to go and have arranged for the jet."

No. Her heart lurched. "Of course you do. I'm so sorry this has happened. Those poor men and families. What can I do to help?"

"I contacted Enzo. He'll be here at two to help close things up and get you to the airport so you can fly home to Domodossola."

"Please don't worry about me. I'll be fine."

He shook his head. "This wasn't the way I planned for the rest of this week to go."

"Accidents happen, Stefano. You think I don't understand?"

"That's the thing. I know you do, thank God. Where's your phone? Besides Enzo's, I'm putting in the number at the main office at the mine in case you can't reach me and there's an emergency here at home." When that was done, he gave it back to her and grabbed his suitcase.

She walked him downstairs. Wind almost knocked her over when he opened the door before they hurried to the car. "I wish you didn't have to fly out in this."

"Don't worry. This is nothing." He tossed his bag into the back seat, then turned to her. "I'll call you after I've arrived and give you an update."

"Please be safe."

"You took the words right out of my mouth, *Signora* Casale." He gave her a long, hungry kiss, then got in and shut the door.

She watched through tear-filled eyes until she couldn't see him anymore.

That kiss had reduced her to the lovesick wife she was fighting hard not to be. Little did he know he was taking her heart with him before she went inside the chalet where she'd known the greatest happiness of her life.

Her thoughts were reeling. The last thing she wanted was to go home to the palace. A part of her had hoped he would ask her to fly to Mexico with him. How ridiculous was that?

When she got upstairs she called her Zia Ottavia. Everyone believed she and Stefano would be on their honeymoon in the Caribbean until the end of the week. No one would be the wiser if she spent time with her aunt. Hopefully, by then, Stefano would be able to fly home and they would arrive at the palace together.

Her mother's older sister was the best friend she'd ever had. She answered on the second ring. *"Pronto?"*

"Zia Ottavia? It's Lanza."

"Lanza! Are you calling from the tropics?"

"No, no. It's a long story, but you can't tell a soul. Are you up for a visitor?"

"How soon?"

"Today."

"*Ehi?* I don't understand."

"I'll explain later, but only if your invitation is still open."

"I want you to come anytime. You know that!"

Lanza was on the verge of tears. "Thank you for being so wonderful. I probably won't be at your house before evening. I'll take a taxi. *Fino a tardi*, Zia."

She hurried to the bedroom and phoned the airport. There was a flight to Rome at four-thirty. If Enzo got here on time, she'd be able to make it.

Once she'd made the reservation, she phoned him and he assured her he would be there by two at the latest. After she hung up, she started packing and made her bed.

Then she fixed breakfast and cleaned up the kitchen.

At quarter to two she turned off the fire-place switch and went downstairs with her bag and coat. Enzo had just pulled up to the door. He did a quick final inspection of the chalet before they left for the city.

"Stefano is so lucky to have a friend like you. I really appreciate your helping me."

"I'm delighted to do something important for him. He was very worried about leaving you alone."

"I'm the one who's worried. A mine cave-in is so awful. If anyone dies, I know he'll take it on."

"He will, but he can handle anything. I've found that out over the years."

When they reached the airport, he walked her inside with her bags. She turned to him. "You've done enough. Please don't think you have to stay with me."

"I want to and I promised Stefano I'd wait till you boarded your flight. I told him I'd arrange for someone from the palace to meet your plane."

"No, no, Enzo. That won't be necessary, but thank you. I'm flying to Rome to stay with my aunt. She invited me to stay with her at the wedding. Now I'm taking her up on it."

His eyes widened.

"I'm hoping Stefano will be back in time for the two of us to arrive at the palace together."

"I see."

They walked to the gate for the flights going to Italy. "Please don't tell him. When he calls me, I'll let him know I'm in Rome."

His eyes danced. "Your wish is my command, Your Highness."

She laughed. "Don't you dare *Your Highness* me! Since our marriage I've forgotten all about being titled. If I'd had the courage to tell my father I didn't want to live a royal life, I would have been long gone like Stefano."

Enzo's demeanor underwent a drastic change with that comment. He looked nonplussed over what she'd said. Lanza decided she could confide in him a little more.

"Stefano and I had to give up our dreams when we were forced to marry, but we've worked out a solution that gives us as much freedom as possible to do our own thing without question.

"Under circumstances that could have spelled the end of happiness for both of us, we've found the perfect way to have freedom and I couldn't be happier," she asserted, keeping a smile pasted on her face while she was in agony. "I believe he's happy, too. Of course I could be wrong. You've been his friend forever and would be the best judge of that."

He went quiet just as her flight was announced for boarding. She jumped up from the seat and gave him a peck on the cheek. "Thank you for being such a good friend to him. Stefano loves you like a brother and I'll never forget your kindness."

It was after 8:00 p.m. when the driver from the Casale mine picked up Stefano at the Ruiz airport outside Zacatecas. He drove him to the mining office, which was on a high plateau that rose to eight thousand feet. The temperature was in the thirties. He felt right at home in the cold air as he walked inside to meet with his other mining officials.

Dozens of workers and family members milled around while Jose Ortega, the chief engineer, apprised him of everything that was happening. Teams of workers would be working through the night taking turns trying to reach the three trapped victims using the latest equipment. Safety inspectors were still trying to piece together why there'd been a collapse in the structure in the first place.

Stefano was determined to find out why all their precautions to avoid such an accident had failed. So far this had never happened before at any of his mines. He'd been proud of the safety records and would be devastated if there was a loss of life.

He stayed in the office where he could sleep on a cot in the back room. To his relief Alicia hadn't shown up tonight. He planned to avoid her if it was at all possible and got to work at his desk.

First, he needed to look over the plans of the mine where the cave-in had happened. Many factors had to have been in play, including the strength and weight of the soil combined with the porosity and amount of moisture.

When he checked with the environmental factors like weather conditions, he discovered there'd been some ground uplifting and tilting two months ago along the Acapulco Trench that included the Tehuantepec Ridge. His mine couldn't be found in fault, but right now he was more concerned that the miners would be rescued.

As the men came in and out giving him updates, he made a call to Enzo, wanting to know how everything went before he phoned Lanza. It was 11:00 p.m. here.

"Sorry, Enzo. I know it's the middle of the night for you. I haven't called Lanza yet because I wanted to talk to you first."

"She's fine. What I want to know is, how

are you? Have the trapped miners been rescued?"

"We're just getting started, but I want to know about my wife."

"I only have one thing to say. She's not the person I thought she was."

Stefano sucked in his breath. "Is that good or bad?"

"What in the hell do *you* think? I steered you wrong when you asked me for advice in my office that day. Before I put her on the plane, I called her *Your Highness*. She forbid me from ever saying that to her again." Stefano chuckled. "She's nothing like what I'd conjured in my imagination."

He closed his eyes tightly. Amen to that. "I owe you, *amico*."

"Good luck and come home safe. *Ciao*."

"*Ciao*."

Relieved with that report, he phoned Lanza while no one needed to talk to him.

To his satisfaction she answered after the first ring in an anxious voice. "Stefano?

Are you all right? What about the trapped miners?"

"Yes and yes. As for the miners, I'll find out soon. There are three of them, but it's going to be difficult reaching them and could take longer than I'd hoped."

She moaned. "Now that you're there to investigate, how do you think it happened?"

"I know exactly what caused it. The graphs showed there was a noticeable ground settling of the earth after tremors along the Acapulco trench a couple of months ago. The collapse couldn't have been prevented."

"Thank heaven you can't be blamed."

"But I will be anyway, and won't be happy until the miners are found and able to be home with their families. I bet your parents were surprised to see you arrive early without me. When I know more, I'll email your father to explain."

"Please don't," she begged.

He frowned. "Why not?"

"I didn't go home, Stefano. I flew to Rome and am staying in my Zia Ottavia's villa. I adore her and she's being wonderful to me. I plan to stay here until you're able to return. If you don't mind, I'd rather meet you at the Domodossola Airport when you fly in from Mexico. We'll arrive back at the palace together."

That explained his conversation with Enzo. She'd mentioned going to her aunt's before. Enzo couldn't have talked her out of it and she'd sworn him to secrecy.

Stefano grinned. His wife was her own person in every way and heavenly shape. "I'm glad you're safe and happy. I'll try to get back as soon as I can."

"Thank you for calling and letting me know you got there without incident. I'll pray those men get out alive."

He swallowed hard. "That means a lot, Lanza. I'm hoping to see you soon. *Buona notte, sposa mia.*"

After hanging up, he left the office to join the other rescue workers. The next few desperate days and nights would keep him from reliving those moments on the couch before Lanza had pulled out of his arms. She'd been life to him, but he had to correct that remark and admit, she *was* life to him.

CHAPTER TWELVE

THOUGH LANZA LOVED spending time with her aunt, her mind wasn't off Stefano for a second. Other than two text messages that said they were still searching for the men, she'd had no other news.

By the fifth day she couldn't stand it. She had to talk to him! But first she called Enzo, who told her he hadn't heard from Stefano, either.

Lanza was fretting that Stefano might feel he had to go down the mine. She had no doubt his life could be in danger if he did and there was another tremor that caused more cave-in. The thought of losing him was too horrendous to contemplate. If she could just hear his voice…

After dinner she went to her room and phoned him on his cell, something she'd promised herself not to do. It was night there. All she got was his voice mail. Lanza hung up, but she couldn't stand not knowing anything.

On impulse she called the mining office number he'd programmed. Someone would be able to tell her what was going on if they were there. She pressed the digit and waited for the call to go through. After a moment, *"Bueno?"* said a female voice.

"Buenas noches, señora. Is there someone in your office who speaks English? I need information."

"Sí."

Frustrated, she said, "I need to speak to Señor Casale, please."

"No disponible," she rapped out.

Thanks to the Spanish she'd learned from one of her tutors, Lanza realized that meant Stefano wasn't there and squeezed her phone tighter. "This is Señora Casale. Will you ask him to call me when he can?"

She could have sworn a half minute passed before she heard the woman say, *"Sí."*

After that one word there was a click that cut them off.

It had to be the shortest phone call in history. Beside herself because she still had no information, Lanza clicked off. The woman hadn't been of any help and probably didn't know English or Italian, but maybe the situation there was as desperate as Lanza had feared.

She hardly slept that night. If she didn't hear from him tomorrow, she would see if her father could get answers she couldn't.

Lanza's prayers had eventually produced results.

Six days after the cave-in, all three men had been rescued to cheers and tears. They would soon be released from the hospital.

Stefano got the cleanup underway and wound up his affairs. At last, he was able to fly straight to Rome to pick up his wife. Six days away from her was too long. He'd gotten used to being with her. Nothing or no one would ever take her place.

En route to the jet he phoned her. "Lanza?"

"Stefano!" she cried. "I've been out of my mind with worry. Thank goodness that woman in the office got my message to you."

"What do you mean? What woman?"

"I phoned last night and a woman answered, but she said you were unavailable. I asked her to tell you to call your wife."

Alicia…

He knew she'd been around, but he'd avoided her. She'd paid him back by not giving him the message from Lanza.

"I would have been difficult to find, but none of it matters. I have the best news! The men are all out and safe. I'm on my way to Rome."

He heard a break in her voice. Hopefully, she was glad he was coming for her. After a minute she said, "How soon do you expect to land?"

"At six-fifteen p.m. your time. Can you meet my plane at the airport?"

"Of course."

"Our families will never know we weren't in the tropics all this time."

"I'm afraid I don't have a tan like yours," she murmured.

"Your ski tan is enough for everyone to be fooled."

She was being too quiet. He imagined she was nervous about them returning to the palace to begin their life together. The best thing that could have happened had been for them to be alone at the chalet. He wished they had another two weeks of freedom ahead of them.

"How's your aunt?"

"Amazing. We've always been close."

"One day you'll have to invite her to the palace to spend some time with us."

"I'd love that."

This chitchat was driving him crazy. "Do you have any news to share?"

"Yes!" All of a sudden she came alive. "I called the refuge. The man who helped us said Fausto adapted well and yesterday they

254 THE PRINCESS'S NEW YEAR WEDDING

took him out in the woods. This morning he didn't come back."

"That means he's found a way to survive."

"I know. I'm really glad. We know he'll be happy now."

Stefano gripped his phone tighter. "How do you feel about that?"

"Fausto is back home. What more could we ask?"

"We couldn't."

He heard her sigh. "You've got a long flight ahead of you."

"Not too bad. I'll sleep most of the way. We'll have dinner on the plane for the short flight to Domodossola. Now I have to go. We're getting ready to take off. See you tonight."

"Be safe."

"You, too."

He hung up and climbed the steps, anxious to get back to Lanza. After chatting with his pilot and steward, he walked to his bedroom. Once they'd attained cruising speed and the seat belt light had gone off, he prepared to pass out until it was time for the descent.

The whole nightmare of the cave-in was over and his wife would be meeting him at the airport in Rome. Maybe now he could actually get some sleep.

Stefano couldn't believe it when the steward knocked on his door and told him it was almost time to fasten his seat belt. He really had needed the sleep. They were about to make their approach.

He shaved and freshened up, then slipped on the same gray suit he'd worn the night they'd left on their honeymoon. His pulse picked up speed as he moved to the club car to check on the dinner menu and get ready for the landing.

The jet taxied along the tarmac. The second it came to a stop, he leaped from his chair. His steward opened the door so he could rush down the stairs.

Like magic, Lanza stepped out of the taxi parked nearby. She, too, had chosen to wear the same suit with the lace hem. She'd even done her hair up with the same pearl clip and the necklace he'd given her. Princess Lanza Rossiano was in evidence once more.

He drew closer to her, noticing a nerve throbbing at the base of her throat where the pearl lay. She was even more beautiful than he remembered when they'd said goodbye at the chalet. Those blue eyes met his for a breathless moment.

Stefano wanted to crush her in his arms, but this wasn't the place in front of his staff or the taxi driver. Instead, he pressed a kiss to her cheek and cupped her elbow. "Come on. Our dinner is waiting for us."

He helped her up the steps and inside to the club compartment of the jet. The steward brought her coat and luggage. After she sat down and fastened her seat belt, he did the same and before long they were in the air. The moment they could unbuckle, the steward served them a pasta dinner with shrimp.

"I told him to serve us soon because this flight won't take us long."

She started to eat. "You asked me earlier if I had any news. I decided to wait and tell you what my aunt told me. She said that while we were gone, my parents had the second floor of the east wing of the palace restored to a home for us.

"It has three bedrooms, a kitchen, sitting room, den, an office with the latest computer software for you, a terrace, two bathrooms, a living room, everything we could want. It's their wedding gift to us."

"That's very generous of them. I'll thank them as soon as possible. Now I'd like some advice from you."

"What is it?"

"I have to fly to Argentina the day after tomorrow. The timing is terrible since I've just returned from Mexico."

She didn't react to the news, but he knew it came as a surprise that he was leaving again so soon. "This meeting with my engineers in Puerto San Julian in the northwestern part of the country was planned before Alberto died and can't be changed."

"Father wouldn't expect you to."

But what about you, Lanza?

"We've been putting in a new process, which increases the purity of gold by electrolysis. I won't bore you with all the details, but by use of an electric current the gold can be restored to a highly pure metallic state, leaving the impurities separate."

"It sounds complicated."

"More than that, it takes time to make sure it's all working satisfactorily and has involved some engineers from Chile, Bolivia and the States. I have to be there to oversee everything. Yet, I know your father is expecting to meet with me in the morning to discuss what responsibilities he expects me to start handling. I'm concerned he'll be offended when I tell him I have a prior commitment before I can give him quality time."

She finished her coffee. "He'll understand. How long will you be gone? Four, five weeks?"

"It could be that long."

"Then tell him the truth and say you'll

probably need five weeks before you're back. That way he won't have expectations you can't meet."

Stefano nodded. "That's sound advice I'll take to heart. I'm sorry I'm going to have to leave you the moment we're back."

She stared at him in a way he couldn't tell what she was thinking. "We knew this would be our life."

Yes, he knew, but he hadn't counted on being crazy about his wife. "What will you do while I'm gone?"

A small laugh escaped her lips. "What I've been doing for several years. I organize benefits to raise money. At present my efforts are for our various homeless shelters. As I told you earlier, there's a new low-income housing project going up on the other side of the city. I'm anxious to get enough money donated to start a soup kitchen.

"And after that, I'm planning to find a billionaire who might be willing to donate land for the building of new housing for our naval vets. Again, it all takes money and sometimes I reach out to our allies who are willing to invest a little."

He heard what she was saying, but she wasn't the same woman he'd been with at the chalet. It was as if she'd lowered a shield between them he couldn't get past.

In several prior conversations with her, she'd told him her sister Donetta, who wanted to be king, would make a great one. To Stefano's mind Lanza was the sister who would make the best ruler.

The steward came in to remove their trays. After he left them alone Stefano said, "I phoned your father's chief assistant, Marcello, earlier and told him we'd be arriving shortly."

One delicate brow lifted. "I would love to have shown up unannounced, but you did the right thing and will be in his good graces. My father dislikes surprises."

"So does mine. Any other advice to help me?"

"You don't need it. Do you know what he said when he told me you'd asked for my hand? 'Lanza? Prince Stefano was raised like his brother, Alberto, and will make a splendid husband for you. His brilliant business acumen is known around the world. He's Basilio's son, after all.' There could be no greater praise."

But Stefano knew Lanza hadn't believed what her father had told her about him at the time. That was because he'd hurt her too deeply.

Our life will begin after we meet at the altar. Don't worry about our wedding night. We'll spend it away from everyone while we sort out the rules of engagement.

Looking back on what he'd said to her crushed him now.

The fasten seat belts sign flashed on.

She smiled at him. "We're almost home. Happy New Year, Stefano."

The waiter poured Lanza more coffee after a working dinner with Matteo Fontana at a

restaurant in the western part of Domodossola City. Earlier in the day she'd walked
through the new low-income, three-story
housing facility with him. She enjoyed
working with the young, good-looking,
wealthy businessman in charge of oversee-
ing this big project, one of her pet projects.

"It's fabulous. How soon can it be opened?"

His warm brown eyes played over her.
"One week, Your Highness."

"You've accomplished everything in such
a short time. I'm awestruck."

"I'm glad you're delighted. Our office is
pleased, too."

"Did you have a chance to look over my
ideas for a series of soup kitchens? I'm still
working on getting the funds, but what do
you think?"

"I went over them with my architect,
Marco. They're brilliant and desperately
needed. If you give me the go-ahead, they
can all be built within six months."

"Wonderful. It will make a big difference
to the problems in this area of the city. I'm

running another couple of fund-raisers in the next two weeks. Hopefully, we'll go over the top with donations and I can phone you with the good news."

To her surprise he suddenly got to his feet, staring beyond her. "Your Highness!"

Who on earth was Matteo addressing? She turned in the chair and almost fainted to see Stefano standing behind her. With his dark hair and eyes, he was so incredibly striking, and looked so handsome in a navy business suit, she could hardly believe that it was her husband standing there.

Stefano had only been gone ten days and wasn't expected back from Argentina for at least three more weeks! She got to her feet. "Stefano—"

Her husband's dark, penetrating gaze took in Matteo before focusing on her. "I got through early with my project and hurried home. Marcello told me I could find you here."

She was in shock. Not only had he come home ahead of time, he'd also gone out of his way to find her. If she wasn't clutching the edge of the table, her legs wouldn't support her.

"L-let me introduce you to Matteo Fontana," she stammered. "He's the dynamic businessman in charge of the fabulous housing project I told you about. We've been talking about the date for the opening."

"It's an honor to meet you, Your Highness." She could tell Matteo was flat-out intimidated because Stefano wasn't only the crown prince, he also had a sophisticated aura that made him stand out from other men.

"My wife has talked a lot about this project. I'm pleased to meet the man responsible."

"The privilege has been mine to work with her. She's one of the most enlightened people I've ever met."

He was very kind. "Thanks, Matteo."

"I couldn't agree more," Stefano murmured before he flicked his gaze to hers.

"Have you finished your business dinner, or shall I come back for you later?"

"We're through, Your Highness," Matteo rushed to assure him. Then he smiled at Lanza. "Let me know about those fundraisers and I'll give Marco the okay to start drawing up the blueprints."

"You're talking about the soup kitchens?" her husband wanted to know.

Matteo nodded.

Stefano eyed her intently. "You've accomplished a great deal in the time I've been gone."

"Your wife is a dynamo and so easy to work with." Matteo looked at her one more time. "Thank you for meeting me for dinner."

"It was my pleasure. *Buona notte*, Matteo."

He nodded to Stefano. "Your Highness. If you'll excuse me."

As he left the restaurant, Stefano put a hand on the back of her chair. "Are you through eating?"

"Yes."

"Then let's go back to the palace. I have the limo waiting."

She walked through the restaurant with him. When he helped her into the back, she could smell the scent of the soap he used in the shower. Her desire for him was off the charts. He sat next to her. With a sideward glance she could see he'd either shaved on the jet, or he'd gone to the palace first to freshen up before coming to get her.

The sun had set as they drove through the city, a magical time with the lights turned on. They hadn't had snow for at least a week, which made it easier to walk around the building site with Matteo.

"How did the process go in Argentina?"

"Good. I felt confident to leave earlier than planned. Tell me how long you've known *Signor* Fontana."

She blinked. "We met about a year ago at a state dinner at the palace when the plans for the project were only in the embryo stage."

"Do you meet with him often?"

"I've seen him dozens of times in the past year and almost every day for the past week."

"Are you aware he's crazy about you? I didn't see a wedding ring."

Was it possible Stefano had developed husbandly feelings for her, and that was why he'd come home early? Lanza's heart almost jumped out of her chest.

"He's not married."

"It seemed to me he forgot you were married, too, until he noticed me walk over to the table."

"Why do you say that?"

"He was eating you alive with his eyes. I'm not sure it's a good idea for you to meet alone with him."

She felt a fluttering in her chest, but chose not to respond to that comment because deep down she knew Matteo did have a tiny crush on her. But more important, she'd never seen this domineering side of Stefano before.

Lanza had thought often about her short conversation with the woman at the mine.

Stefano had played dumb about it, never letting on who it was. Perhaps she'd been one of the women he'd once had an affair with.

That relationship might be in the past, but he'd come home to Lanza, who was still unfinished business. Was that it? Could that be the problem challenging him? Was she his only failure when it came to seducing a woman? Her thoughts darted hither and yon.

Before long they reached the palace and the driver took them around to the east entrance. Stefano helped her out of the limo. A staff member opened the large palace doors so they could walk up the steps. Once on the second floor, they entered their apartment, the size of the average person's house.

Ten nights ago he'd gone to one of the bedrooms to get some sleep early because he'd had to leave for the airport at five o'clock the next morning. Lanza had stayed up to talk to her sisters about her trip and hadn't gone to bed until one in the morning in another of the bedrooms.

Tonight was different.

Stefano was in a strange mood she didn't understand unless she was right and he hadn't liked seeing her with another man. Had it brought out his egotistical side, and now he was feeling possessive? If so, it wasn't enough for her.

He removed his suit jacket and undid the top buttons of his shirt where she saw a dusting of black hair on his chest.

After he pushed his sleeves up to the elbows, he hunkered in front of the fireplace to put more logs on the fire. While it crackled and the flames lit up the semidark room, she couldn't take her eyes off his well-honed physique. Right now she was having to fight overpowering feelings of desire for him.

She stood near the long, rounded green velvet couch facing the fireplace. Its color was reflected in the background of the huge tapestries hanging on the walls depicting medieval forest scenes with animals.

"Why didn't you phone that you were coming tonight, Stefano? I would have planned to have dinner waiting for you."

He stood up and turned to her, putting his hands on his hips in a totally male stance. "I wanted to surprise you and take you out for a meal."

"That would have been very nice. I couldn't believe it when Matteo called out and said, 'Your Highness.'"

"I know for a fact he wasn't happy to see me."

"You're wrong, you know. It's just that you're bigger than life to everyone and it intimidates them, even Enzo, who worships you."

"You're mistaken."

"No, Stefano. I witnessed it with my own eyes."

Maybe that was true, but Lanza had been deeply engrossed in conversation with Matteo when he'd walked into the restaurant. Even from a distance, Stefano could tell the man was totally entranced with her.

At that moment Stefano had experienced a flare of jealousy, which was so foreign to him, he'd felt violent inside. What made it worse was that Lanza seemed to enjoy Matteo's attention. Seeing them together like that had disturbed him so much he couldn't seem to calm down.

She was always gracious and charming with a style all her own, but Stefano had felt deflated that she hadn't shown more excitement at seeing him tonight. Ten days away from her had felt like death.

"My father will be thrilled to know you're home."

"He already knows. We talked for a moment and I've been asked to have breakfast with him and your mother."

Lanza smiled. "She's anxious to give you a tour of the stables and the kennel. She is an animal lover like me and my sisters."

"I'm sure that will be enjoyable, but aren't you going to come with us?"

"I can't. While you've been gone, I've had a full schedule of duties. Tomorrow I have to leave early enough to visit a school of students at risk by eight in the morning.

I'm making an assessment of their needs in order to gather donations of books and other supplies they lack."

He admired her work ethic more than she would ever know, but he missed the intimacy of the chalet. It seemed that nothing was the same here at the palace.

"I understand, but now that I'm back, I'd like to spend more time with you. We need to coordinate our activities."

To his disappointment, Lanza simply smiled and said, "I agree, but could we leave it for now? I'm dead tired after a full day and need to get to bed."

"Don't go yet— We have to talk."

"Can't we do that tomorrow after I return?"

She seemed so distant. He longed for the closeness they'd had in the chalet.

"No. This can't wait."

Her brows furrowed. "What's wrong?"

He rubbed the back of his neck absently. "I don't like what's happening to us."

"Because I wasn't here when you flew home from Argentina?"

"That and other things."

"Oh." Lanza looked perplexed. "If you don't mind me asking, why do you care? We both agreed to do our own thing, no questions asked. I can't help it that you came home from your trip early. Now you're breaking your own rules. Which is it, Stefano? You can't have it both ways."

Frustrated beyond reason, he reached for her, pulling her against him. "I cut my trip short by three weeks because I missed you and couldn't get home fast enough. I want us to have a real marriage."

Lanza pulled away and looked at him, confused.

"No, you don't," she argued back. "You made it clear to me from the start that this was going to be a business arrangement."

"I know," said Stefano, sighing. "But I do now, and I think you want it, too. When you kissed me back at the chalet, I knew you

274 THE PRINCESS'S NEW YEAR WEDDING

wanted me even though you wouldn't admit it. It's not something you can hide."

Lanza moved out of his arms, cutting him to the quick. Her eyes stared at him as if she didn't know him.

"What's happened to you? I can't believe you could change this fast without a reason. Does this have anything to do with my father? Don't tell me he demanded that we produce an heir before the year is out? Is that what this is all about?"

"Lanza—"

How could she think that? But then again, he had never spelled out to her that his feelings for her had changed. No wonder she wouldn't listen to him. She carried on in full flow.

"Is that why you came home early? Did you feel guilty? Or did my father insist you hurry home to get me pregnant ASAP?"

As it happened it was Stefano's father who had brought it up during a phone conversation he'd had with him while he'd been in Argentina. He'd been upset that Stefano had barely come home from Mexico before flying off to South America so soon. "How can you and Lanza have a family under these circumstances?" he'd complained, and Stefano had had to admit he was right.

Her cheeks were flushed, and he could see she was agitated and upset. "When I agreed to marry you, I was planning on normalcy until you warned me of your rules of engagement and told me ours would be a marriage of convenience. It killed something inside me."

He groaned. Why had he sent her that note? "I know that now. I was so wrong and I'm sorry I've hurt you. I would love to start again. Please, can you forgive my foolish mistake?"

"It's not a case of forgiveness, Stefano. I guess I'm not like other women. My sisters tease me for being naive and gullible. They reminded me that this is a business arrangement, even if I let myself believe for a time in the chalet it could be more than that. But you managed to take off my blinders. If you

want to try for a baby tonight, let's do it!"
Stefano looked at her in shock. Had he really made her feel like this? He felt ashamed
that he had hurt her so badly.

"You deceived me with this marriage and
were my second choice. Not that I actually
had one."

Stefano tried to protest, but she had started
for her bedroom. When she reached the
door, she turned around. "Well? Are you
coming to fulfill your next duty to produce
an heir? Let's get it over with."

Minutes passed before Lanza realized Stefano wasn't going to follow her. She went
into the bedroom, but before the door closed,
she saw that the color in his face had turned
ashen. She felt so sick and heartbroken, she
wanted to die.

Heaven help her. What had she done?
While he'd stood there begging her forgiveness, she'd cut him off.

In reality he *had* come home from Argentina much earlier than planned. Stefano had

told her he'd missed her. He'd displayed a jealousy she couldn't have imagined when he'd found her with Matteo. But she'd dismissed all that. She'd been angry with him and lashed out, but now she felt terrible for the way she must have hurt him. She'd seen the stricken look on his face as she'd left the room.

Lanza stood with her back against the door, burying her face in her hands while the tears gushed. How could she have let her pain turn her into someone she despised? What she needed to do was beg *his* forgiveness.

Without hesitation, she left the bedroom and hurried across the apartment to his bedroom, praying he hadn't left the palace already. He would have had every right.

"Stefano?" When he didn't answer, she knocked. There was no response so she opened the door. In the semidarkness she saw him sitting on the edge of the bed with his head bent and his arms clasped between his powerful legs.

She was so thankful he hadn't gone, she hurried toward him. Standing in front of him she said, "Stefano? Can you ever forgive me for what I said to you? I didn't mean any of it." Her voice throbbed.

He lifted his dark head and looked up at her. "There isn't a cruel bone in your beautiful body. You spoke the truth when you said *I'm* the one who deceived you. What frightens me is that you'll never believe I've fallen in love with you. I love you, Lanza. So terribly in fact that I don't know myself anymore."

She knew those words had come straight from his heart and she launched herself at him.

"Darling—" She threw her arms around his shoulders. "Can you ever forget the awful things I said to you? I can't believe I said them. I love you so much I can hardly breathe. By the time we took the carriage ride on our wedding day, I knew I loved you because I'd already had help from Alberto."

"What do you mean?" he whispered against her throat.

"Your brother idolized you. When you asked what he and I talked about when we were together, most of the conversation was about you. He told me story after story and wished he could be half the man you were."

"He said those things?" Stefano sounded incredulous.

"Yes, and much more. He made me fall for you long before I met you at the altar. But I fought my feelings with all my might because I never dreamed his brilliant, dashing elder brother could ever fall in love with me."

"*Lanza*—"

Stefano didn't give her a chance to say another word. He followed her down on the bed and began to devour her, kissing away her tears. She lost all sense of time and surroundings as they attempted to assuage their longing for each other. Being loved by her husband was absolute heaven.

Lanza had been convinced she'd never find love, or never know how it felt to be adored and ravished by a man like Stefano, who was worshipping her with his body.

The rapture he brought her was beyond anything she could have comprehended. They gave each other continual pleasure throughout the night and morning. In their euphoria, they forgot the world and only sought to bring each other joy.

"Have you really forgiven me, *bellissima*?" It was midmorning and he'd tangled his hands in her hair. "I was out of my mind to say and do what I did to you."

She kissed his mouth hungrily, never able to get enough of him. "To be honest, I was shocked you would actually marry me after you'd given up the royal life for so many years. I still can't believe you went through with the wedding. I'm the luckiest woman on earth."

He cupped her face in his hands. "There's something you need to know that will explain why I agreed to our marriage." In the next breath he told her about Alberto's sacrifice. As the story unfolded, tears welled in her eyes once more.

"Oh, Stefano—that explains the picture he sent me of you."

His gorgeous dark eyes filmed over. "You were right, *amore mio*. There was no man more honorable and I was a coward for running away as long as I did. When I found out he never intended for me to know what he'd done for me, I knew I had to follow through in his place. But what I don't understand is why you were willing to marry me."

"I have a secret, too. One I hope won't upset you too terribly."

"Now that I know you love me, I'm too happy to be upset about anything."

She covered his face with kisses, loving him to distraction. "When my parents told me you'd asked for my hand and that they wanted me to marry you, I rebelled until they told me my father had a health problem. They still haven't explained exactly, but I'm pretty sure it's his heart. *Papà* told me he needed a son-in-law to lean on."

Stefano kissed her long and hard. "I already knew."

"But you couldn't! They didn't tell anyone."

"My father figured it out during a visit two months before our wedding and told me Victor was slowly fading. When I heard that admission, I thought that if the woman I was about to marry could love her father enough to make a sacrifice that earthshaking, then I had to have faith that we could eventually make a good marriage. But like you, I fought it hard in the beginning. The day my parents told me I had to marry you, I went to see Enzo and get his advice."

An impish smile broke out on her succulent mouth. "What did he say?"

"You want the exact translation?"

"You know I do."

"He said, 'All right—there's only one way I can see this working. You need your freedom, so do her the biggest favor of her life and yours. You've got a year before the wedding. Let her know *before* you're married that you plan to be your own person and continue doing the mining work you love while you help her father govern. It'll mean you'll be apart from her for long periods. Give her time to adjust to that fact, know what I mean?'"

Lanza burst into laughter first. "I love Enzo. When he drove me to the airport, he was surprised that I was flying to Rome. I told him you and I had to give up our dreams when we were forced to marry, but we worked out a solution that gives both of us as much freedom as possible to do our own thing without question. To think that little monkey was the architect of your rules of engagement."

"In a manner of speaking." Stefano grinned before kissing the hollow in her throat.

She kissed him back. "I also told him our circumstances could have spelled the end of happiness for both of us, but we found the perfect solution through freedom and I couldn't be happier. Enzo must be laughing his head off about now."

Stefano pulled her on top of him and looked into her eyes. "I talked to him the other day. He told me he thinks I'm the luckiest man on the planet and I better be good to you. What he didn't know was that I already wanted you beyond reason."

So saying, he covered her mouth with his own and gave her another long, passionate kiss that went on and on. When he finally lifted his head he whispered, "You have no idea how much I missed you. Every night when I went to bed, I dreamed of you. The next time I have to leave, I'm taking you with me."

"Darling—"

"Just promise me one thing."

"What is it?"

"That you'll forget that letter I sent you and the things I said to you on our first morning at the chalet. I'm in love with you and plan to be so good to you, you'll love me forever."

Her eyes shone like hot blue stars. "Is that your way of saying you believe in forever?"

"You've convinced me there's something

to it because I can't imagine life without you. When you went to the other bedroom last night, it felt like death. I never want to experience that feeling again."

"I know because I felt it, too. That's why I came flying back into you. Thank you for forgiving me."

She burrowed her face in his neck. "I love you, love you."

"Enough to have my baby?"

"Oh, Stefano—I can't wait to get pregnant."

"We'll have beautiful royal babies because you'll be their mother." He bit her earlobe gently. "Do you think they'll hate us for bringing them into the world?"

"They'll get over it."

"How do you know?"

She gave him an illuminating smile. "*We* did."

* * * * *

LET'S TALK

Romance

For exclusive extracts, competitions
and special offers, find us online:

 facebook.com/millsandboon

 @millsandboonuk

 @millsandboon

Or get in touch on 0844 844 1351*

For all the latest titles coming soon,
visit millsandboon.co.uk/nextmonth

Want even more
ROMANCE?

Join our bookclub today!

'Mills & Boon books, the perfect way to escape for an hour or so.'

Miss W. Dyer

'Excellent service, promptly delivered and very good subscription choices.'

Miss A. Pearson

'You get fantastic special offers and the chance to get books before they hit the shops'

Mrs V. Hall

Visit millsandbook.co.uk/Bookclub and save on brand new books.

MILLS & BOON